09-ABF-321

The Boy Who Could

FLY

Robert Newman
Illustrated by Paul Sagsoorian

AN AVON C CAMELOT BOOK

AVON BOOKS
A division of
The Hearst Corporation
959 Eighth Avenue
New York, New York 10019

First Camelot Printing, August, 1976
Third Printing

Printed in the U.S.A.

For Jennifer and Ethan

The Boy Who Could

FLY

1

"WAIT HERE," SAID GRANDFATHER. "I'LL BE RIGHT back."

We were in Grand Central station, standing at the bottom of the marble stairs that led up to one of the balconies. I watched him go over to the ticket window, then looked around. When we had first come in, walking through the waiting room, Joey and I had paused. I had expected everything in New York to be big. But somehow—maybe because the building wasn't as tall as lots of others and had looked kind of old-fashioned on the outside—its size inside had surprised me. As usual, however, Grandfather had been in a hurry, and we had had to hurry, too, as we followed him over to the information booth.

But now that he had checked on the train and relaxed a bit, we could relax, too. The part of the station that we were in was huge. The ceiling was several stories up and it was vaulted and painted blue and had all the signs of the zodiac on it. Opposite us was an advertisement: a color photograph of flamingoes that was bigger than a billboard. There were shops everywhere. And besides the regular stairs and the ramps there was a wide moving stairway that was taking people up into the Pan Am building and bringing others down into the station.

I glanced at Joey. His eyes were very bright, the way they usually get when he's interested in something. But he wasn't looking at any of the things I was looking at. He was watching a man trying to open one of the metal lockers near the stairs. The man was apparently in a hurry, like almost everyone around us, because he kept looking at the clock over the information booth and swearing under his breath as he twisted the key. But it wouldn't turn.

"Not 5241," said Joey finally. "5244."

"What?" The man scowled at Joey over his shoulder, but he took out the key and looked at the number on it, then tried it in the locker to the right. It turned easily, and the door opened. He took out a suitcase and swung around.

"How did you know that?" he asked. "How did you know I was at the wrong locker?"

Joey didn't answer, and I moved over to stand closer to him. I knew how he knew, but I couldn't tell the man because he wouldn't have believed me. That's one of the troubles with having a kid brother like Joey—you have to keep coming up with explanations for things he's done that people *will* believe. But before I could say anything, the man said, "It doesn't matter. Thanks anyway." And he went trot-

ting off toward one of the gates.

I sighed.

"Joey . . ." I said.

"I know," he said. "But he only had three minutes, and he was afraid he was going to miss his train. I'm sorry." But he didn't look sorry. He looked as if he thought it was funny. And since in a way it was, I grinned and so did he.

By this time Grandfather was walking back toward us with the tickets, and, while I'm not Joey, this was once when even I knew what someone was going to say before he said it.

"Look, your grandmother and I don't *have* to take that flight this afternoon, you know. I mean . . . are you sure you'll be all right? That you can manage?"

It was the third time he had asked that since we had left the airport.

"Yes, Grandfather," I said, trying not to sound impatient. "I'm sure."

He frowned down at us, but it was a worried frown, and suddenly I didn't feel impatient anymore. I knew how he felt. Even though it would mean losing a whole day if he came with us, he was concerned about letting us go the rest of the way by ourselves. On the other hand, he didn't seem to understand how Joey and I felt. That we were looking forward to the train trip, and looking forward to it all the more because we *would* be making it alone. But finally he must have realized it because—

"All right," he said abruptly. "The track's over there."

"Come on, Joey," I said.

We picked up our flight bags and went to the gate. There was a sign there listing the stations at which the train stopped. Westfield was about two-thirds of the way down. I hoped Grandfather would say good-bye to us before we went any farther, but of course he didn't. He went through the gate with us, down the ramp, and on board the train. It was an old train and rather dirty. He settled us in one of the coaches, gave me our tickets, and then said, "You know when we're due back, don't you?"

"In March."

He nodded. "Even your grandmother should have had enough of Europe by then. We'll come up and see you first thing and, if you're not happy for any reason and want to come back home with us, you know you can."

"We know, Grandfather," I said.

He stood there for a moment. He wasn't frowning, but he still looked fierce—the way he did when he was upset about something. I knew he didn't like saying good-bye and leaving us, but at least he wasn't going to cry about it the way Grandmother had.

"Well," he said. "I guess I'd better run along. Good-bye."

He shook hands with me, patted Joey on the head, and left. There was a conductor outside on the plat-form, and when Grandfather went over and talked to him, the conductor looked through the window at us. Grandfather was evidently telling him to keep an eye on us, make sure we got off at Westfield. And while I didn't know why he had to, if it made him feel better it was all right with me. We were on our own at last, Joey and I, at least until we got to West-field. And I was glad.

We sat there, looking around and enjoying the idea of being on a train, because with all the traveling we had done, we had never been on a train before. We had flown from New Mexico to Los Angeles, and of course we had just come East by plane, too.

There weren't many people in our coach to begin with, but more kept coming in, and by the time we left, about half the seats had been taken. We started with a jerk, moved slowly along the platform and into the darkness beyond. Almost everyone in our coach was either reading or just sitting there, not bothering to look out, as if there was nothing to see. But there was.

A shiny steel train went past us, going the same way. It was all lit up and there were lots of people in it, some sitting in the dining car, some in small rooms and some in the parlor cars. When it disappeared, we seemed to be the only thing that was moving in that mysterious underground world. We could see tracks running off into the distance with red, yellow, and green lights shining next to them, and several times we passed other trains, not moving but still and dark like herds of sleeping elephants. What made this part of the trip even more exciting was to know that we were traveling under the streets —streets that were busy and full of traffic with people walking on the sidewalks and, towering above them, all the tall buildings we had seen when we circled over the city before we landed at the airport.

Then suddenly we left the tunnel and were out in the sunlight. It was even more interesting now because the tracks were up above the street and there were houses on both sides of us, so close that you could see into them. We saw people eating, and a man standing at an open window and shaving with an old-fashioned straight razor, and several times we saw kids sitting out on the fire escapes or playing there as if they were on a terrace or a balcony. Joey was quiet, as usual, taking it all in. We stopped at a station that was high up over the street, and a few more people got on, and then we went on again.

A few minutes later, after we had gone over a bridge and were rattling along in a kind of open cut, the conductor came through. It was the same conductor Grandfather had talked to, and when he took our tickets, he said he'd tell us when we were getting to Westfield. He smiled at us, particularly at Joey, but he didn't look at him the way people do sometimes.

I've never been sure why people look at Joey that way, as if there was something odd about him. Of course, he is different—different from anyone I've ever known—but you can't tell just by looking at him. At least most people can't, because most people don't really look at other people, just as they don't really listen. He's about average height for his age and has reddish brown hair and freckles, but then so have I. Maybe it's because of his eyes. They're grey and very large, so large that they make his face seem small, and they change. Sometimes, when he's thinking about something, they get quite dark. And other times they're very clear and seem to have almost no color, like water.

I guess I've always known in a vague sort of way that Joey is different, but I still remember the first time I really thought about it, saw him through someone else's eyes. It was when he was not quite two years old and I was nine and we were still living in New Mexico. Dad was home—it was the last time they let him come home from the hospital, about a month before he died—and we were just about to have dinner. I remember how Dad looked, very pale and thin, and I remember that Mother was very quiet, probably because he did look that way. I sat down at the table, and Mother asked me where Joey was. I said I didn't know, and I didn't—I'd been over at a friend's house all afternoon. When I got up again a minute later, she asked me where I was going.

"I'm going to get Joey," I said. "He's down in the cellar."

"The cellar?"

"Yes."

"I thought you didn't know where he was."

"I didn't. But he just told me."

"What do you mean, he told you? I didn't hear anything. Did you, Paul?" she asked Dad.

Dad shook his head.

"I can't help it," I said. "That's where he is. He went in and the door blew shut and he can't open it. I'll be right back."

I went out and around to the back of the house and pushed open the cellar door—it always stuck—

and there he was. He smiled at me, that slow smile of his, and I helped him up the steps and we went into the house together.

"Were you in the cellar?" Mother asked him as he climbed up on to his chair at the table. He nodded and she turned to me. "Did you lock him in there?"

"Of course not," I said.

"Then how did you know where he was?"

"I told you," I said. "He told me."

"That's ridiculous!" she said, starting to get angry.

"Easy, Marjorie," said Dad. He was looking at us rather strangely, first at Joey and then at me. "Maybe Joey did tell him."

"What do you mean?" Mother asked. "How could he?"

"I don't know," Dad said. "But I know Mark isn't a liar."

Of course, there had been other times before that —one time in particular that was a kind of family joke. That was when Joey was only a few months old. He had been crying, and no one seemed to know why until I went into his room and raised the window shade, so he could look out. And when he stopped crying, and Mother asked me how I knew that was what he wanted, I said the same thing: "He told me." She and Dad had both laughed about it then and whenever it came up afterwards.

But that later time, when Joey had been in the cellar, Dad didn't laugh. I think he may have known. I don't think he knew everything, just how different and special Joey was. I'm not sure I knew myself— it took a while for me to realize what it meant. But I think Dad knew then that there was something between us. That Joey could always tell what I was thinking—just as he could tell what anyone was thinking—and that I could tell what Joey was thinking. When he wanted me to know, that is. And I think it made Dad feel good to know that there was this thing between us and also to know how we felt about each other.

I came back to the present. Being Joey's brother had always meant problems for me and I had an idea that there were going to be even more of them in the future. But I decided not to think about that now. I wanted to enjoy the train ride.

We were well out of the city by this time, and the train was moving right along. In fact, we actually seemed to be traveling faster than when we were in the plane. I suppose that's because when you're in a plane, flying very high, you can see things a long way off and it takes a while to get to them and pass them. But here everything was very close—telegraph poles and houses and trees—and since we went past them quickly, we seemed to be traveling fast.

There was a highway running along beside the tracks, almost as wide as one of the Los Angeles freeways, but there didn't seem to be as much traffic on it as on the freeways. Then, off to the right, we saw water—very blue water—the Sound. There were lots of boats out, some with white sails and some with brightly colored ones, and once we even caught a glimpse of a lighthouse.

Shortly after we left the Sound and had started going inland, a man came through the train with sandwiches, candy, and drinks. He was short and kind of hunched up and kept blinking as if he was sleepy. He reminded me of someone, but I couldn't decide who.

"Mr. Mudge," thought Joey.

The things Joey thinks often make me laugh, and I started to laugh now, but I caught myself.

"Stop that!" I said, jabbing him with my elbow. Mr. Mudge was an old groundhog who lived up in the hills where Grandfather used to take us on picnics. Joey had named him Mr. Mudge, and he was right—that's who the man did look like. Because I felt awkward about it—almost laughing, I mean— I decided we ought to buy something. Joey doesn't like chocolate, in fact, he rarely eats anything sweet, but I got him a bag of nuts and bought orange drinks for both of us.

We were due to arrive at Westfield a few minutes after four. About three o'clock the train stopped and changed engines. We'd had an electric locomotive before, but now we had a diesel. We went on again, the locomotive whistling a good deal for crossings. It was a sound that might have seemed rather sad and lonesome if you were feeling that way yourself, but neither Joey nor I did feel that way, and we both liked it. The country had changed again and had become rather rolling. Though it was the end of summer, the grass was still quite green, and we began to see cows grazing in the fields or lying in the shade under the trees. Some of the trees, tall and spreading, were different from the kinds we were used to, but Joey knew they were elms and maples.

Since we were going to be spending at least a year in Westfield and maybe more, the nearer we got to it the more interested we became in the countryside. There was a river close to the tracks. It was wide and full of rocks and small islands. We crossed it several times, clattering over iron bridges, and it was still in sight when the train began slowing up for Westfield.

The conductor came into the car to tell us to get ready to get off, but by then we had already taken our flight bags down from the rack overhead. When the train stopped, we were the first ones off.

Joey and I saw Aunt Janet and Uncle George at the same time. We had come to know them quite well during the past few years. They had been out to visit us in our place in New Mexico, and again later on when we were living with Grandfather and Grandmother in Los Angeles. As a matter of fact, they'd made a special point of coming out the three summers after mother died. But, even if we had never seen Uncle George before, we would still have known him. He was a little taller than Dad and, since he was a few years older, his hair was getting gray, but he still looked very much like Dad. He had the same thin face and rather sharp nose, and he stooped a little just as Dad had. It had always seemed to me that he and Aunt Janet both looked a bit sad at times. Of course, there was good reason for them to look that way after two deaths in the family—first Dad and then Mother. But Joey thought that wasn't all. He thought that part of the reason they were sad was that they didn't have any children of their own.

But they didn't look sad now. They were standing on the platform of the station and, when the train stopped and they saw us coming down the steps, they came hurrying over. Aunt Janet hugged and kissed first Joey and then me, and Uncle George shook hands with us both.

"How was the trip?" he asked.

"Fine," I said.

"No problems?"

"No. No problems."

"Good," he said.

Then Aunt Janet hugged us both again.

"We're very glad you're here," she said. "Terribly glad."

When she let go of me, I caught a glimpse of Joey's face. He was looking around and his eyes were large and dark. I don't know about Joey, but when I want to know what he's thinking I have to kind of reach out. In other words, I don't follow what's going on in his head all the time; if I did, I'd never have a chance to think anything myself. And sometimes, if he's not actually trying to tell me something, what I get isn't too clear. That's the way it was now. He wasn't really *thinking*, but he seemed to have a feeling that something was going to happen here in Westfield—something he didn't like. And I found that a little upsetting—not because he was necessarily right—but because, as far as I knew, he'd never before had a feeling about something that was *going* to happen.

2

OUR BAGS HAD BEEN CHECKED THROUGH, AND I
went with Uncle George to get them. The baggage
man knew him and said hello and, after Uncle
George had introduced me, he said hello to me, too.
We took the bags out to the car where Joey and Aunt
Janet were waiting for us. The car wasn't new, but
it seemed in good condition, probably because Uncle
George was a science teacher, so of course he knew
all about cars.

We drove up a wide street from the station to the
Green. It was quite a large Green, and it looked very
much the way I had thought it would look. There
was a Civil War monument at one end of it and a
bandstand at the other and in between were trees
with benches under them. Most of the houses were
large and white with cupolas on top of them and
porches either in front or on the side. Even the stores
that were scattered around the Green were white and

looked Colonial, though they weren't old.

The school was at one corner of the Green; Uncle George pointed it out to us as we went past it and up a tree-lined street.

The house was a few blocks from there, on top of a hill. It wasn't quite as large as some of the houses on the Green, but it was white and had a porch, and there was a red barn behind it that Uncle George used as a garage.

Joey and Aunt Janet went into the house, and I helped Uncle George with the bags. When we went inside, I found that the house was also very much the way I had expected it to be. There was a hooked rug on the wide plank floor at the foot of the stairs, and opposite the stairs was the parlor with the dining room and kitchen in back of it.

I went up the stairs behind Uncle George. At the top he opened a door and said, "We thought we'd give you this room, Mark."

"What about Joey?" I asked. "Where will he be?"

"In here, right next to you."

He opened the door between my room and the one next to it. Joey was already in there, standing in the middle of the room, looking around.

"How did you know this was your room, Joey?" Uncle George asked him.

"You told us," said Joey.

"Did I?" He looked a little surprised. "I don't remember. As a matter of fact, your aunt and I only talked about it for the first time this morning. Not that it matters. I'll give you a chance to unpack. Then, if you're hungry, I've an idea there may be a little something waiting for you in the kitchen."

He went downstairs again, and I looked at Joey through the open door. Neither Uncle George nor Aunt Janet *had* said anything to us about our rooms, but one or the other of them must have been thinking about it, so of course Joey knew.

I glanced around as I opened my suitcase and began to put my things away. It was a good-sized room, a little larger than Joey's, and quite sunny. There was a bed in it, a chest of drawers, a desk and, between the windows, a bookcase full of books. It suddenly occurred to me that since Dad and Uncle George had lived here when they were boys, these must have been their rooms once. I wondered which one had had which room, and discovered that Joey was thinking about that same thing. He felt that he had Dad's room and I had Uncle George's. Later on, when I asked about it, it turned out he was right. In the meantime it gave me a strange feeling—strange but good—to think that we were going to be living in the same rooms in the same house that Dad and Uncle George had lived in when they were our age.

I finished unpacking and went into Joey's room. He hadn't even started to unpack. Instead, he was over near the window, looking out. I looked out, too. There was another house close by. It was white and had a porch, and while we were standing there, the back door opened and a girl came out. She was wearing jeans and seemed to be about my age. She picked up a hoe and started to work in the vegetable garden that was in the rear of the house.

"Do you think you're going to like it here?" I

asked Joey, remembering the incident at the station.

He nodded.

"Yes, they are nice," I said, meaning Uncle George and Aunt Janet, which was what he was thinking about. Then, "Look, Joey, you're going to have to be careful from now on. I don't mean what just happened about the room. I mean you're going to have to talk more instead of just thinking things. Grandma and Grandpa were used to your not saying very much. But Aunt Janet and Uncle George aren't used to it, and they'll be sure and notice."

"All right," he said.

"I'll help you unpack," I said.

"All right," he said again. But before I even had his bag open, I could feel him begin to slip away. He was starting to think about the trees and the grass and the flowers. I couldn't quite follow it, but it had something to do with the fact that they seemed to grow more naturally in the East than they did out in New Mexico or Los Angeles, possibly because there was so much more water.

After we had finished putting his things away, we went downstairs. Aunt Janet was in the kitchen, and Joey must have remembered what I said because when she asked us if we'd like some cookies, he said, "Yes, please."

They were ginger cookies, homemade and not too sweet. Joey didn't say anything about them, but he didn't have to because Aunt Janet could tell how much he liked them, and she looked pleased. I had three of them and a glass of milk, and then I said I thought I'd go outside and look around. I asked Joey if he wanted to come with me, but he said no, that he'd stay with Aunt Janet and that seemed to please her, too.

The girl next door was still working in the vegetable garden. I expected her to pretend she didn't know I was there until I did or said something to attract her attention and then to do a take and act surprised. But she didn't. As soon as she saw me standing at the fence, she put down her hoe and came over. She was slim and had dark hair and was quite pretty.

"You must be Mark Haynes," she said.

"That's right."

"I'm Sally Martin. Your aunt and uncle have talked about you a good deal. They said that you and your brother were coming here to stay with them."

"We just got here a little while ago."

"I know," she said. "I saw you drive up. Did you take the two o'clock train?"

"Yes."

"It's not much of a train."

"It wasn't bad. Not that I'm any judge. I've never been on a train before."

"You haven't?"

"No."

"But you must have trains out in California."

"Oh, sure. I just never happened to be on one. Except in Disneyland, and that wasn't really traveling. It's just kind of a ride."

I sometimes have trouble talking to girls, especially when they either act coy or come on strong the way some of them do. But she was so easy and natural that I had no trouble talking to her.

"How did you know I was from California?" I asked. "Did Uncle George and Aunt Janet tell you that, too?"

"Yes. They said that you've been living out there with your grandparents, but they were going away so you were coming here to stay with them."

"That's right. They've gone to Europe. Grandma and Grandpa, I mean."

Her face lit up. "That's exciting. I'd love to go there sometime. I've never been. Have you?"

"No," I said. "But I've got an aunt who's been living there for a couple of years now."

I told her about Aunt Helen whose husband is with the State Department and about her new baby, which was one of the reasons Grandma and Grandpa had gone to London. We talked about school, which would be starting in two days, and it turned out we were both in the same grade and I said I hoped we'd be in some classes together, and she said she hoped so, too. Then she asked me the same thing I had asked Joey.

"Do you think you're going to like it here?"

"Of course."

"That's good."

There was something a little odd about the way she said it.

"Don't *you* like it?" I asked. "Living here, I mean."

"Why, yes. I guess the trouble is I've been living here all my life, and every once in a while I feel as if I'd like a change, something different."

I nodded. I could understand that. On the other

hand, I'd had lots of change. More than I needed.

"Is that why you want to go to Europe?" I asked.

"Part of the reason." She looked past me. "I guess that's your brother, isn't it?"

I turned, and there was Joey, standing looking at her. I said yes and introduced them and she smiled at him. Joey just looked at her for a moment, then he smiled, too, and that made me feel good. I wanted her to like Joey and Joey to like her, and it was clear that they did like each other. I decided that Joey had been wrong to feel that something bad was going to happen. In fact, I didn't see how anything bad could happen. Joey could do a lot of things, but I didn't think he could predict the future.

The rest of the day was very pleasant. The more I saw of Aunt Janet and Uncle George, the better I liked them. Of course, we had known them quite well before, but sometimes people are different at home, especially when you're living with them.

We sat around talking for a while after dinner. Occasionally, in the past I had talked to Grandpa—especially when he was taking us somewhere and didn't have other things on his mind. But somehow talking to Uncle George was even better—partly because he was younger, nearer Dad's age, and partly because he knew a lot of things that Grandpa didn't. Anyway, I liked it.

I was tired after all the traveling, so I went upstairs shortly after Aunt Janet sent Joey up. He had listened to us talk without saying very much, and I was anxious to see how he felt about Westfield, Uncle George, and Aunt Janet now.

I went into his room. He was in bed, but he wasn't asleep.

"He's worried about something," he said.

"Uncle George?" I was pleased that he had remembered to say it instead of just thinking it even if we were alone, but I was also a little surprised. "He didn't seem worried to me."

"Well, he is."

"About us?"

"I don't think so."

"Well, grown-ups often worry about things. Grandpa used to worry about business and Aunt Helen and Grandma's rheumatism. And as long as it doesn't have anything to do with us, our being here . . ."

"I don't think it has," he said. "He and Aunt Janet are both glad we're here."

"Well, that's the important thing, isn't it?"

He nodded. I said goodnight and went back into my room, but I was a little concerned. As far as I knew, Joey had never been wrong about people, and if he said Uncle George was worried, he was. And since he wasn't absolutely sure, I couldn't help wondering if perhaps it *didn't* have something to do with us.

Joey and I both slept well. Uncle George and Aunt Janet were in the kitchen when we went downstairs the next morning, and we all had breakfast together. After breakfast Uncle George asked us if we'd like to take a drive, see something of the country, and Joey and I said yes. It was a warm, sunny day, a good day for a drive.

"I thought you had some work to do," said Aunt Janet.

"You mean the report? I'll do it this afternoon," said Uncle George. "I'm not trying to get the boys off by myself. You can come along with us if you like."

"No thanks," said Aunt Janet, smiling. "You go ahead. But don't get home too late, and don't buy them anything that will spoil their appetites for lunch."

"I wouldn't dream of it," said Uncle George, winking at us.

We drove north, away from Westfield and into the country. Uncle George told us that though they had once raised a good deal of tobacco in the area, it was mostly dairy country now. We stopped a few times to look at some farms, watch a hay-baler working and see them filling a silo. Then we circled around over some dirt roads to see a covered bridge, one of the few left around, and finally ended up back in town.

Uncle George wanted to get something at the drug store, and he parked on the Green near the school. I looked over at the building, and when he saw me looking at it, he said, "What do you think of it?"

"The school? Why, it looks all right."

It was a four story, yellow brick building with a playground and ball field behind it.

"Yes, I suppose it does. It was quite a good school when your father and I went there."

"You mean it's that old?"

I looked at it again, more closely, and now I could

24

see that the steps outside were worn and the doors cracked and peeling.

"Yes," said Uncle George. "Not that that's important; there are much older schools around. It could use some repair work. But what we really need is another school."

"Another one?"

"A separate high school. Because, as things stand now, we're getting so crowded that we'll probably have to go into double sessions next year."

"Hello, George," said a voice behind us.

We both turned. A tall, thin man wearing steel-rimmed glasses was standing there.

"Oh, hello, Frank," said Uncle George.

"Still collecting material for your report?"

"No," said Uncle George. He smiled, but it seemed to me that his smile was a little forced. "I was just showing the school to my nephews. This is Mark, and . . . Where's Joey?"

"Over there," I said, nodding to where Joey was standing on the far side of the Green. "Shall I get him?"

"Don't bother," said the man. "I'll probably be meeting him, or at least getting a look at him, during the next week or so."

"Mr. Burton is the school principal," explained Uncle George.

"Yes, I'm the chief ogre around these parts," said Mr. Burton. "Or at least one of them. I hope you're not going to be too disappointed in us. The school, I mean."

"I'm sure I won't be," I said.

"Really? Maybe I ought to get that in writing. Be seeing you, George."

Uncle George looked after him thoughtfully as he crossed the street and went into the school. Then, realizing I was watching him, "What's Joey doing?" he asked.

"I don't know," I said.

We went across the Green and found that Joey was staring at a small, dark boy who was sitting on a bench under one of the big elms.

"Oh, hello," said Uncle George. "You're Luis Ramirez, aren't you?"

The small, dark boy nodded.

"Your brother was in one of my science classes last year." Then, indicating Joey, "Have you two met?"

I had a feeling that neither Joey nor Luis had said a word so far, that they'd just been looking at one another. But they both nodded.

"That's good," said Uncle George. "What's your brother doing these days?"

Luis pointed toward the drug store without saying a thing.

"That's right. I remember hearing he was working there. We were just going to go in and get some ice cream cones. Would you like to come in and have one with us?"

Luis glanced at Joey and, though it was clear he was a very shy boy, he nodded again.

"Fine. Let's go."

Aunt Janet was in the kitchen when we got home

and she wanted to know where we'd gone, what we'd done.

"Oh, we just drove around, ended up in town."

"Did you meet anyone?"

"Yes. We ran into Frank Burton."

"Oh?" said Aunt Janet. "How was he?"

"Strange," said Uncle George.

"What do you mean?"

"We met him in front of school, and he wanted to know if I was still collecting material for my report."

"He was joking, of course."

"Let's say half joking."

"I see," said Aunt Janet.

Neither of them said any more, but from the look on both their faces, I began to think that perhaps Joey had been right when he said Uncle George was worried about something.

After lunch Uncle George disappeared into his study and Joey and I went out to do some work in the garden with Aunt Janet. First we did some weeding, and then we helped her pick tomatoes. Some of them were small cherry tomatoes, and when I asked Aunt Janet if we could eat some, she laughed and said of course. That it was no fun picking anything unless you ate some.

We were on our way back to the house when a station wagon pulled into the driveway. It was a brand new one, very big and shiny. The man driving it got out, and so did the boy who was with him—a boy about Joey's age. The man was quite a bit older than Uncle George. He was heavy set and had a big jaw, something like a bulldog's, and a thick shock of white hair. He looked angry, but I had a feeling that he wasn't angry about anything in particular, that he looked that way all the time. He didn't say hello to Aunt Janet or even nod to her. He just said, "Is George around?"

"Yes, Wally," said Aunt Janet. "He's in the house."

"I want to see him," said the man, and without asking if it was all right, without asking anything, he went clumping up the steps and into the house.

"Who's that?" I asked.

"Wally Jordan," said Aunt Janet. "The First Selectman."

"What's a First Selectman?" I asked.

"Very much the same thing as a mayor. There are three selectmen who manage the town's affairs, and the First Selectman is the most important of the three."

"Oh," I said. "What do you suppose he wants to see Uncle George about?"

"I'm not sure. George is on the local PTA, and he's been working on a report to be presented to the school board. It may have something to do with that."

"You don't like him, do you?"

"Who?"

"Wally Jordan."

She glanced at me, hesitating a moment. "No, I don't. He's been giving your uncle a hard time."

"About what?"

"Well, he didn't like it much when George became the teachers' representative on the PTA board. And he liked it even less when your uncle began working on that report. George has been very patient about it.

Sometimes I think he's been too patient. In fact . . ."
She broke off, "I'd better go in. Do you want to take
the tomatoes around and leave them at the kitchen
door?"

She went into the house, but I didn't rush to do
anything about the tomatoes. The boy who had
gotten out of the car with Mr. Jordan was standing
there and looking at Joey. He was a little taller than
Joey and huskier, and he had the same sort of bulldog face as Mr. Jordan. That may have been one of
the reasons I felt the way I did about him. Because I
didn't like him before he ever opened his mouth, not
that that took him very long.

"What's your name?" he asked Joey.

Joey Haynes, thought Joey.

There he goes again, I thought. Sometimes Joey
forgets that he can't just think things when he's with
anyone besides me, that he's got to say them.

"I asked you what your name was!" said the boy.

"I said Joey Haynes."

"What do you mean, you said? You didn't say
anything!"

"I'm sorry," said Joey.

He'd been studying the other boy while the other
boy looked at him. Joey doesn't take dislikes to people the way I do, but he does decide people aren't
interesting, and that was how he felt about this boy,
so he turned and started to walk away. As he did,
the boy shoved him. At least, he tried to shove him.
But even though Joey's back was to him, Joey knew
what the boy was doing, or thinking of doing. He
stepped sideways, half turning at the same time, and

the boy went past him, tripping over one of Joey's feet and falling face down on the grass next to the driveway.

He lay there for a moment, the wind knocked out of him. It served him right, but I thought I'd better do something about it so I started toward him. As I did, he caught his breath and began to cry. He went on crying even after I picked him up, and he was still crying when the door opened and Mr. Jordan came hurrying out.

"What is it, Eddie?" he asked. "What happened?"

"He did it!" said Eddie, pointing at Joey. "He knocked me down!"

Mr. Jordan stiffened, looking first at Joey who was standing there quietly, his eyes wide, then at the crying boy who was at least half a head taller than Joey.

"He knocked you down?"

"Yes," said Eddie. "And hard, too!"

"No, he didn't," I said. "He tried to shove Joey, and when Joey stepped aside, he tripped and fell."

Mr. Jordan looked at me now, and his face was red and angry.

"Are you calling Eddie a liar?"

"No," I said. "But I was right here, and I saw what happened."

"Who are you, anyway?"

"Mark Haynes. And this is my brother, Joey. We're staying here with Uncle George."

Mr. Jordan looked at Joey again. Then, "All right," he said to Eddie. "Stop crying. I'll take you home."

"But, Grandpa . . ." said Eddie.

"I said stop crying! Come on." And taking Eddie by the arm, he hustled him over to the station wagon, got in himself, and drove off. Aunt Janet and Uncle George had come out of the house with Mr. Jordan, and they were standing on the porch.

"That really is what happened, Uncle George," I said.

"I'm sure it is," said Uncle George. "I know Eddie."

"I'm sorry about it," I said. "I mean, I hope it's not going to make any trouble for you with Mr. Jordan."

Uncle George smiled crookedly. "It won't," he said. "At least it won't make things any worse. Wally Jordan and I aren't exactly friends. We haven't been for some time."

"Because of your school board report?"

"How did you know about that?"

"Well, Mr. Burton mentioned it this morning. And Aunt Janet just said something about it, too."

"Oh. Yes, I guess it's partly that and partly a matter of chemistry. Or maybe zoology. We're not the same breed of cat."

"Cat and dog would be more like it," said Aunt Janet. "Though I'm normally quite fond of dogs."

"All right, Janet," said Uncle George. "You weren't hurt, were you, Joey?"

Joey shook his head.

"Good. Then let's forget it. But watch yourself with Eddie. He's got a mean streak in him, and I'm afraid he's not just a bully, he's a bit of a sneak."

"Well," said Aunt Janet. "That's something new."

32

"What is?"

"Saying that about Eddie."

She seemed glad he had said it, and so was I. I knew Uncle George liked kids, but that didn't mean he had to like every single one of them, even the jerks.

3

"SOME MORE LEMONADE, MARK?" ASKED MRS. Martin.

"Maybe just a little, thanks," I said.

It was about ten o'clock at night, and I was sitting on the Martins' porch with Sally and her mother. We had gone to a band concert after supper—Uncle George, Aunt Janet, Joey, Sally and I—and had only gotten back a short while before. Uncle George and Aunt Janet had told us quite a bit about Westfield the times they had come out to visit us, but they had never said anything about a band concert, so I had no idea of what it would be like. Lights had been strung up on poles and between the trees, and folding chairs had been set out in a circle around the bandstand. All the grown-ups and the younger kids sat there. But the older teen-agers sat farther away, on the grass or the benches or in the cars that were parked around the Green.

The band wasn't exactly a symphony orchestra, but they didn't try to play anything but marches and popular things, and it was very pleasant to sit out under the stars and listen to the music. During the intermission most of the younger kids had run around, buying popcorn and ice cream. Joey hadn't, but when he saw Luis Ramirez a few rows ahead of us with his folks and his older brother and another Puerto Rican family, he had gone over and sat with them for a while.

The whole town, even the drug store, was dark when the concert ended, and the high school kids who had cars began driving off, almost all of them going in the same direction. I asked Sally where they were going, and she said that since there was nothing to do and no place to go in Westfield, they were driving to hot dog stands and pizza places on the Branford road.

Sally's mother was on the porch when we got home, and she waved to Uncle George and Aunt Janet and asked if they'd like to visit for a while. They thanked her and said no, but that I could if I wanted to.

So there we were, and the lemonade was very good. Dr. Martin, Sally's father, was on the telephone when we arrived, but he finally came out and joined us. I'd met him before, when I called for Sally. He was very brusque and direct, but I liked him.

"How's your uncle?" he asked me, taking a glass of lemonade.

"Why, fine," I said.

"That's good," he said. "I haven't really had a chance to talk to him in some time. He's a good man."

"Of course he is," said Mrs. Martin. "And a good teacher. They were lucky to get him back in school again."

"Back in school?"

"Why, yes," said Dr. Martin. "He taught school here before he left to do research with Northeast Instrument in Branford. He's only been back teaching for about three years now. And a good thing, too. That he's here now, I mean. At least I hope it's going to be a good thing."

"Now don't get started on that, Sam," said Mrs. Martin. "Mark's not interested in Westfield politics."

"Yes, I am," I said. "Especially if Uncle George is involved."

After everything that had been said, I really did want to know what it was all about.

"Oh, he's involved all right," said Dr. Martin. "I don't think he wanted to be, and he wasn't at first, but he is now."

He explained that Westfield had grown quite a bit during the past few years and that when Uncle George began teaching again he had found that the school wasn't what it had been, that it was getting crowded and run down, and that some of the good teachers were starting to leave because the salaries were so low.

"He did say something this morning about a new school," I said. "Why haven't they built one?"

"Because of Wally Jordan," said Dr. Martin.

"Now, Sam," said Mrs. Martin.

"All right. Because building a new school, doing most of the things your uncle would like to see done, would cost money. Which means the tax rate would have to go up a point or two. And there are quite a few people in town, Wally Jordan in particular, who don't care what else happens as long as that one thing doesn't."

"How do you think it's all going to come out?"

"I'm not sure. As I said, your uncle didn't want to get involved in all this. All he wanted to do was teach. But he did get involved. He's well liked and very much respected here, and ever since he became active in the local PTA, he's been getting a lot of support. On the other hand, Wally Jordan's been in office for a long time, and he's a pretty tough customer. He's put the heat on several people who should be for the PTA program. Frank Burton, for instance. He's the school principal."

"Yes, I know," I said.

"I think Frank would like to back your uncle, but he's afraid to. I'd say the program has a fifty-fifty chance of going through. A lot depends on what the school board does about the new budget. And *that* depends on how they react to a report your uncle's been working on."

"You're always telling people more than they want to know, Sam," said Mrs. Martin.

"It wasn't more than I wanted to know," I said.

"You mean you understand all that?"

"Kind of," I said. "At least I know who's for Uncle George and who's against him and why."

"That's a good beginning," said Dr. Martin.

School started the next day. Sally and I had arranged to walk to school together, and she stopped by at about twenty to nine. Uncle George had left by then, but she said good morning to Aunt Janet, and then the three of us—Sally, Joey and I—set off down the street. We kept running into other kids, some our age, some older and some younger, and Sally made a point of introducing Joey and me to them. I couldn't remember all their names, but I knew I would in a day or so.

Sally showed us where Joey's classroom was, and I took him in. His teacher's name was Miss Gregory, and she was young and attractive and seemed very nice. Apparently Uncle George had talked to her about Joey because she knew all about him and introduced him to the rest of the class. They all seemed quite friendly, except Eddie Jordan, who I should have realized would be in Joey's class. He didn't exactly scowl at Joey, but he certainly didn't look as if he was delighted to see him again. On the other hand, Luis Ramirez was in the class, too; and when Joey saw him, he went over and sat next to him. Joey doesn't always pick the friends other people would, but he usually has a good reason for liking them.

Sally took me up to our room, which was on the second floor. Mrs. Tyler, our homeroom teacher, was an older woman who looked as if she could be quite strict, though she was pleasant enough to me. She told the rest of the class who I was and that I was from Los Angeles, and then said she was sure I would have some interesting contributions to make. I don't think the rest of the class liked that very much, and I wasn't too happy about it myself. You may be interested in someone who comes from somewhere else, but you don't like to feel that he knows anything that you don't. The same thing had happened when I went from the school in New Mexico to the one in Los Angeles. I'd been able to live it down there though, so I decided I'd probably be able to live it down here, too.

Classes began right away. I hadn't been there in the spring when everyone else had registered, so Uncle George had worked out a schedule for me. This wasn't too difficult since there wasn't as much of a choice in the subjects you could take as there had been in the school in Los Angeles. Even that first day I could see I wasn't going to have any problems with school work. The school in New Mexico had been new and very good, and since most of the students had been the children of scientists and technicians who worked at the laboratories and were very bright, we had learned a lot in a hurry. As a matter of fact, even though the school in Los Angeles was good, too, I found I'd already had most of the material we got there. The same thing was true here. I was well ahead of the class in math, and they were on the American colonies in social studies and I'd already had that; so all I had to do was be careful about letting anyone know what I *did* know. As for the rest—making friends—I wasn't too worried about that. I'd been able to do it before, and there was no reason why I couldn't do it again. The one I really worried about was Joey. He hadn't been to school before—just to kindergarten. And school, even first grade, could make a lot of difference in what happened to him.

Since it was the first day of school, our social studies class was dismissed early, and I went downstairs to see how Joey was doing. The door was open, and I could see Joey sitting near the front of the room with Luis Ramirez. His class was having science, at least the kind you have in the lower grades where you discuss pets and animals and common trees. They were talking about animals children had seen during the summer, and Miss Gregory was asking, "Does anyone know the name of the animal that lives in streams and builds dams?"

She looked around the class and then at Joey.

"Beavers," he thought.

"That's right, Joey," she said. The rest of the class stirred, but she didn't notice.

"And how do they build their dams?"

Again she looked at Joey.

"With small trees," he thought, "that they cut down with their teeth."

"Right," she said. "That's very good."

"What do you mean, that's good?" said Eddie Jordan. "He didn't say anything."

"What?" said Miss Gregory.

"He didn't," said Eddie.

"He didn't say a word," said the boy next to him.

"But he did. At least . . ." She broke off, looking startled and a little puzzled. I knew what had happened because it had happened once or twice before. When someone gets very interested in Joey and looks right at him without thinking about anything else, sometimes that person can get what he's thinking just the way I can. But of course now that the class had made Miss Gregory realize that something strange had happened, she wouldn't be able to do it again.

"I told you to watch it, Joey," I thought. "Will you please be careful?"

He turned around and looked at me.

"I'm sorry," he thought. "I forgot."

I had to leave then, and I could only hope that he'd remember. Because this was one of the things I was afraid of—that he'd forget where he was and with whom. And if he kept on doing it, there'd be trouble.

The rest of the day went by quickly. One of the boys in my home room, Billy Talbot, got a football from the gym teacher, and we passed it around for a while after lunch. He told me that there were class teams and that I'd have a chance to play football—touch, that is—and basketball, which was good news.

I stopped in at Joey's room again after my last class, but Joey wasn't there.

"He went off with another boy," said Miss Gregory. "Luis Ramirez."

"Oh, yes," I said. "They met yesterday."

"So I gathered. I was a little worried about Luis. His family moved up here last spring—there are just two Puerto Rican families in town—so he was only in kindergarten for a few weeks. But I understand he wasn't at all happy."

"Why not?"

"You know how it is being a stranger and coming into a group late."

I nodded.

"I was afraid he might have a difficult time this year too. That's why I was so pleased when I discovered that he and Joey seemed to like one another. He needs a friend—Luis, I mean."

"I guess everyone does."

"Yes. Your brother's quite a remarkable boy, isn't he?"

"Yes, he is," I said. Then, catching myself, "In what way, Miss Gregory? I mean, how?"

"Well, he seems to know a great deal for his age. And I get the impression that he can read already."

"Yes, he can."

"Is that your doing?"

"I guess partly."

"Well, as I said, he's a remarkable boy. There were times when I was a little concerned about this particular class. But now I think it's going to be a very interesting one."

When I got home, Aunt Janet asked me where Joey was and I told her. She didn't really know the Ramirez family, but she knew about them and where they lived so she wasn't concerned about Joey. I wasn't either. Joey could take care of himself better than most kids. And, of course, that's where the danger lay. The only time I did worry about him was when he showed how well he could take care of himself and how much he knew.

I had some homework to do so I went up to my room, and after I was finished, I spent some time looking at the books in the bookshelves. They all had Uncle George's name in them, and they started with fairy tales and a few Oz books and went through *Robinson Crusoe* and *Swiss Family Robinson, Ivanhoe, The Three Musketeers,* Conan Doyle and Jules Verne to books that Uncle George must have read in high school. Among them were copies of *Alice in Wonderland* and *Through the Looking Glass,* which I must have read to Joey five or six times before he could read himself. I've always liked to read and I read a lot, but I don't talk about it much because you never know when someone's going to think it's square or strange or something to read for fun and not because you have to.

About five o'clock I heard Joey come in and I went into his room. I wanted to find out how the rest of the day had gone for him. He was standing at the window, looking out. Since the house was on top of a hill and fairly high, we could see the river that wound its way through the fields on the far side of town. There was corn growing tall in some of the fields and cattle grazing in others. Beyond them were the hills on which we could see farm houses and an occasional large tobacco barn.

"What kind of a day did you have?" I asked.

"Good. I went over to Luis' house."

"Miss Gregory told me. What did you do?"

He shrugged. I know it's not always easy to tell someone exactly what you did do—sometimes it's fun not to do anything—so I didn't ask any more questions about it.

"Look," I said. "What I wanted to talk to you about was what happened when I came down to your room before lunch. You've got to be careful about that. Thinking things, I mean, instead of saying them."

"But it's much easier and quicker than saying them. And Miss Gregory knew what I meant. At least she did until Eddie Jordan said something about it."

"I know. But that made it even worse. More dangerous, anyway."

"Why?" he asked.

"You mean why is it dangerous?" I sighed. "We've been over it a dozen times. Do you remember the pigeons?"

He nodded, his eyes getting very large. There had been a flock of pigeons in the park near our house in Los Angeles, and we used to go over there a few times a week to feed them. One day a new pigeon, a pure white one, arrived and tried to join the flock. And either because it was a stranger or because it was a strange color, all the other pigeons attacked it, pecking at it until it flew away.

It had been a shocking, frightening experience for Joey. He had turned so pale I thought he was going to faint.

"Why did they do that?" he had wanted to know.

I had tried to explain why, but he couldn't accept it then, and it still seemed hard for him to accept it now.

"But they could all do it if they wanted to," he said, "—think things instead of having to say them. Even Eddie Jordan. Luis started doing it almost right away. And even if they can't do it, why should it matter? We're all different. Everyone is different from everyone else."

"Yes," I said, "but we can't be too different. If we are, the same thing can happen as happened with the white pigeon."

"But it's wrong," he said. "It's all wrong."

"I know. But that's the way things are. Or at least the way people are. They don't understand anything that's too different and they don't like anything they don't understand. That's why I keep telling you that you've got to be careful."

He looked at me, thinking about it. He was upset. And once he knew I knew he was upset, he did something he had done only a few times before. His eyes became darker as if something had shut behind them, and he closed his mind, just as you would close a door, so I couldn't get even a hint of what he was thinking or feeling. This upset me, and I didn't know what to do, so I just walked out.

It was still light after supper, and when I saw Sally come out the kitchen door of her house, I went downstairs and ducked under the fence into her backyard, looking for her. I found her sitting on a bench near a flower bed. She had a sketchbook on her lap and as soon as she saw me she closed it.

"I'm sorry," I said. "I didn't realize you were busy."

"I wasn't really."

"Yes you were," I nodded toward the sketchbook. "Can I see it?"

She hesitated a moment, then opened it. She had been doing a sketch of her house. It was almost finished, and it looked awfully good to me. It was not only clean and sharp, but when you looked at it

46

somehow you knew it was a place that people had been living in and taking care of for a long time.

"You didn't do all that just now," I said.

"No. I've been working on it for a couple of days."

"I think it's terrific."

"It's not bad," she said, looking at it. "Of course things are a lot easier to draw than people."

"Why?"

"Because you don't have to show what's inside things, what they're really like."

I glanced at her, a little surprised. That was the sort of thing Joey would have said. And that might have been one of the reasons they had liked each other right away. Because, in a curious way, they were very much alike: both were interested in what went on inside people.

"Is that what you want to be?" I asked. "An artist?"

"It's what I'd like to be. I've been studying with Miss Parker, the art teacher at school, for about a year now. But . . ."

She paused, and I turned around. Joey had come out of the house and into the Martins' backyard too. He was standing near their barn, looking up, and for some reason he seemed rather disturbed.

"Hi, Joey," I said. "What is it?"

"Those swallows," he said.

Sally and I looked up also. Two barn swallows were circling near the open door of the Martins' barn, wheeling up and then down again and giving their faint, high-pitched call.

"It's nothing, Joey," said Sally. "They always fly

around like that at this time of day. It's when they feed."

"No," said Joey. "It's something else." He went in through the open door of the barn and then called, "Mark!"

Sally and I both got up and went into the barn after him. The Martins used their barn as a garage, too, and on the hood of their car was what seemed to be a small bundle of feathers. Joey picked it up and held it out to us. It was a baby swallow, smaller than his hand and still a little too young to fly.

"It fell," he said. "From up there."

Sally and I looked up. There was a nest on the side of one of the rafters almost directly above the car.

"Is there a ladder around?" I asked Sally.

"Over here."

It was pretty heavy, but we were able to lift it together and rest it against the cross-beam under the nest.

"All right," I said to Joey. "Give it to me."

He put the bird in my hand. It was soft and warm, and I could feel its heart beating. Holding it carefully, I went up the ladder. The two swallows were circling even more excitedly now, flying into the barn and then out again and calling whit-whit-whit. When I stood on the cross-beam, some fifteen feet up, the nest was just above my head. There were two other baby swallows in it. I started to put the one in my hand into the nest. Then,

"Here's the trouble," I said, "why it fell. The nest is broken."

The nest was made of mud, stuck to the side of the rafter, and the front part of it had broken off. The two remaining baby swallows were in the back of it and were all right, but I was afraid if I put the one I was holding in the front it would fall out again.

"Clay," said Joey.

"I've got some," said Sally. "Stay there." And she went running off toward the house.

I stood there with the bird in my hand, trying not to think of how narrow the beam was or how high up I was.

"Why do you always get me into these things?" I asked Joey.

"You didn't have to do it," he said.

"Of course I did. I can just about reach the nest. How would you have reached it?"

He shrugged, and I could feel him slip away. He wasn't thinking about me or what I was saying. He was thinking about the mother and father swallow, concentrating on them as if he were trying to make them understand that there was nothing to be frightened about.

Sally came running back into the barn with a lump of clay in her hands, and without hesitating, she climbed up the ladder and on to the beam next to me.

"Here," she said. "Give me the bird."

I gave it to her and took the clay. I guessed that she did modeling as well as sketching because the clay was soft and wet. I broke off a bit, kneaded it into a strip and laid it on the front part of the nest, working it gently into the old, dried mud. Then I took the bird from Sally and put it back into the nest.

"All right," I said. "That should do it."

I followed her back down the ladder to the ground. The mother and father swallow were wheeling around inside the barn now, and their whit-whit was not as agitated as it had been. Joey looked up at them, then at us.

"Thanks," he said.

"Don't thank us," said Sally. "We wouldn't even have known about it if it weren't for you."

"Yes, you would," said Joey. "You were busy talking, and of course that's one of the troubles with talking. But once you stopped, you would have known."

He looked up at the birds again, then turned and went back to the house. I glanced at Sally, expecting her to say, "What did he mean—that's one of the troubles with talking?" But she didn't. She was looking up at the birds, too. And she was smiling.

4

I DIDN'T PAY AS MUCH ATTENTION TO JOEY DURING
the next few weeks as I usually did. In the first place,
I was busy making friends, which in some ways was
easier to do in Westfield than it had been in Los
Angeles. Out there, there hadn't been any kids near
where we lived, none my age anyway, and if I went
home with someone after school, I'd have to be called
for or driven home. But in Westfield, although quite
a few of the kids lived on farms and took the school
bus to and from school, a great many others lived in
town; so I could walk home with them and then walk
back to Uncle George's. At the same time, I was also
playing quite a bit of football. And finally, I was seeing a good deal of Sally. She and Joey and I would
walk to school together every morning. But he would
generally go home with Luis after school or else Luis
would come to our place, so that about the only time
I saw him was just before or after supper, and then I

would have homework to do.

I don't know what Joey and Luis did or talked about when they were together; I'm not sure they did much talking. They were pretty quiet when they were at our place, mostly just sitting in Joey's room. And, while I don't think Luis could read when he and Joey first became friends, he must have learned how very quickly, because later on he almost always had a book in his hand.

Aunt Janet liked Luis, but she used to worry a bit about the two of them. She would come up to Joey's room and ask them if they didn't want to go out and play. They would look at one another and then go out to the barn or the backyard, but after a while, they'd go back to Joey's room again.

It may have been because I wasn't with Joey as much as usual that I suddenly realized one day that what he was thinking about and the way he was thinking had both changed. When you're very young and you're playing in your room, it doesn't matter to you whether the door is open or shut. But as you get older, you become self-conscious and so you start closing the door.

It was the same way with Joey. He didn't shut the door between our rooms; that was always open. But, possibly because I'd talked to him about the white pigeon again, he kept his mind closed a lot of the time so that I couldn't tell what he was thinking about unless he wanted me to. I'd go into his room when Luis wasn't there and he'd be sitting at the window. Of course he'd know I was wondering what he was thinking about, and sometimes he would just smile

and say hello and that would be that. But other times —not too often—he'd let me see the way someone younger than you will open his hand a little shyly to show you something he's just found.

In the past, when he was thinking about a tree, for instance, he would think about only the tree. Now he seemed to think about it in relation to other trees and everything else. It would unfold like a nature film. First there would be the tree alone. Then, like a camera zooming in for a close shot, he would concentrate on a single leaf, studying its shape and the veins in it and tracing the veins through the capillaries in the branch and down the trunk to the roots. Then the field would widen and take in the roots that spread out in very much the same pattern as the veins in the leaf, crisscrossing the roots of other trees and sometimes struggling with them for water or light, but still living with them—all of them affected by the same things: the sun and the soil and water and animals and worms and bacteria. And in the end I'd have a picture of a whole area in which everything played a part and was related to everything else.

But that wasn't all. It was during this time that I began to realize that Joey wasn't just thinking about outside things, but about himself as well—trying to figure out where he belonged in an even more complicated pattern—and I had the feeling that it was beginning to become clear to him, though it wasn't to me. I kept trying to follow his thinking because I had a feeling that if Joey fitted into the pattern in a particular way then I did, too. And although I knew that some day I'd have to understand it, at the moment it was too much for me.

While Joey may not have had much to do with any of the other kids in his class, I knew he liked school and was doing very well there—maybe too well. Several times when I had passed his room I had seen Miss Gregory staring at him as if he had just said something that astonished her, and one day I came across her talking to Uncle George in the hall. She was quite excited and Uncle George was very interested, but he also seemed a little puzzled, probably because Joey was so quiet at home. I waited for Uncle George to say something about it, but he didn't, possibly because he had so many other things on his mind; I gathered from what I heard around school and at home that the whole school question was coming to a head. Then one evening something happened that gave him a better idea of what Miss Gregory was talking about.

Aunt Janet was in the parlor making paper decorations for a party of some sort in the kindergarten. She didn't teach regularly anymore, but she still went in to school every once in a while as a substitute when they needed her to help out. I was talking to Aunt Janet, and Uncle George was reading, when Joey came in. He stood there for a few minutes, watching Aunt Janet, then he picked up her scissors and cut a strip of paper about two feet long and three or four inches wide. He gave one end of the strip a half twist, pasted the ends together so that it made a ring and handed it to me along with the scissors.

"Cut it," he said.

"What do you mean?" I asked.

"Cut it in half," he said.

I didn't know what the idea was, but I began cutting it the way he had indicated—the long way, parallel to the edges—naturally expecting that I would end up with two rings. But instead, when I cut through the last section with the half twist, I found I still had only one ring, half as wide as the original ring but twice as long. I looked at Joey, and he smiled, pleased.

Uncle George had been watching us and now he came over and said, "Do you know what that is, Joey?"

Joey shook his head.

"You mean nobody showed it to you?"

"No."

"Then how did you know what would happen when Mark cut it in half?"

"I just knew."

"Do you know why?"

"Because it's one."

"What do you mean?"

"It's just one," said Joey, gesturing.

"You mean it has just one continuous plane or surface," said Uncle George looking at him strangely. "That's right. It's called a Moebius surface or a Moebius ring. And if you cut across it, it still has only one surface, so it remains only one ring. You're sure no one showed it to you—your father, for instance?" He glanced at me.

"No," I said. "At least, not that I remember."

"Are there any others like it?" asked Joey.

"Other figures, you mean, with the same kind of properties? Well, there's the Klein bottle. Come on upstairs, and I'll see if I can find it for you in one of your father's books."

They went upstairs together to Joey's room and stayed there for quite a while. When Uncle George came down again, he looked more thoughtful than ever. I wondered whether I should say anything to him, but I decided not to. I'd never really talked to anyone about Joey before, and I didn't want to begin now because I wasn't sure how far I should go, how much I should say. I went up about a half hour later and found Joey in bed. He was staring off somewhere, but when I came into the room, he smiled at me and said, "He found it."

"That book of Dad's he was talking about?"

"Yes."

There was a book lying next to him. It seemed to be a book on different kinds of science because some of the illustrations were drawings of atomic structures, some had to do with biology, and some with astronomy. He showed me a page on which there was a sketch of the ring he had made. Next to it was a strange figure that was something like a bottle except that the top was rounded and the bottom curved up and into it, becoming the inside.

"It's a crazy looking thing," I said.

"Yes," said Joey. "But *it's* one also."

"What does it do?" I asked.

He looked at me in surprise. "It helps you *see*," he said.

"Oh," I said. It didn't help *me* see anything, but

apparently it had helped him because when I had come into the room his mind had been open for once and he had been thinking about lines going out into space and then curving around and twisting at the same time in a very curious way. I said goodnight to him, but I don't think he even heard me because he didn't answer.

We played a pick-up game of touch football the next afternoon, and after it was over Billy Talbot and I stayed on for a while fooling around. I was trying some really long passes, and they were working pretty well, so well that Billy had to hustle to get under them. He waved to someone after one of them, and I suddenly realized that his older brother, Tom Talbot, was watching us. Tom was a junior and a halfback on the varsity, one of the best football players in the school.

"That's quite an arm you've got," he said.

"I can't always get them off that way," I said.

"Seems to me you do pretty well," he said.

Billy had joined us by now.

"Thinking of signing him up for the varsity, Tom?" he asked, grinning.

"Not this year or maybe next," said Tom. "But the year after that. . . Are you going to be around here then? I mean, are you going to be staying on in Westfield?"

"I don't know," I said. "It's possible. Why?"

"I think I'll tell Mr. Meecham to keep his eye on you."

Mr. Meecham was the football coach, and even if Tom was kidding, I still liked the idea. Then—

"Who's that?" Tom asked.

I looked up. Joey and Luis were walking past the field on their way to Luis' house. But somehow I knew it was Joey that Tom was asking about.

"He's my brother," I said.

"Oh," said Tom. He glanced at me, then at Billy. "Haven't you had enough for today?"

"I guess so," said Billy. "See you tomorrow, Mark."

They went off together, and I took the ball back into the school. Tom hadn't said anything, but I got the feeling he thought it was a little funny for Joey to be friends with Luis, and I didn't like it—that he had thought that, I mean. Because, while I didn't know Luis well, it seemed to me he was the most interesting kid in Joey's class.

When I left the school, I ran into Sally coming out of the library, and we went into the drugstore and had sodas, so I got home fairly late. Uncle George must have been waiting for me because as soon as he heard the door he came out of his study and said, "Can I talk to you for a few minutes, Mark?"

Whenever a grown-up says anything like that you naturally expect trouble. I didn't know what was up, but no matter what it was, there was nothing I could do about it, so I said, "Sure, Uncle George."

I followed him into his study, which was off the living room. It was a nice room with a fireplace in it and lots of books and some ship models that Uncle George had made. Uncle George sat down at his desk and began filling his pipe.

"We haven't really had much of a chance to talk," he said. "At least, not just the two of us."

"I know, Uncle George."

"Once this darn school thing is settled, maybe we can become more of a family. But in the meantime, how have things been going?"

"Do you mean generally or at school?"

"Both."

"Why, fine," I said. "School's pretty easy. I've already had most of the stuff they're giving us, but I don't mind that. As for the rest, being here's been swell. I like it a lot. And so does Joey."

"I'm glad to hear it. About the school, it's not the greatest, but it's not bad either because we still have some very good teachers. If we get the money we want and can hold on to them, it should make a big difference. But, as you probably know, there are problems involved."

"You mean Wally Jordan?"

"Yes. I guess he's the most important one."

He paused. I felt he hadn't come to the point yet, the real reason he wanted to talk to me. I was sure he didn't want to talk about Wally Jordan. And I was right because now he said, "Mark, you probably know Joey better than anyone else does. What do you think of him?"

"He's my brother," I said cautiously.

"Meaning you like him."

Liking wasn't exactly the way I would have put it but, "Yes," I said. "I like him. I like him a lot."

"I thought you did," he said. "Not that brothers always like one another."

"I know. Some of my friends can't stand their kid brothers. But didn't you like Dad?"

"I more than liked him. Though I'll admit that there were times when I was a little jealous of him."

"Why?"

"Because I think I knew when I was still quite young—about your age—that he was a lot smarter than I was and that he was going to go a lot farther. And of course he did."

"I wondered about that," I said. "I mean, how old Dad was before anyone realized he was kind of unusual. I've known Joey was practically since he was born."

"Oh?" Uncle George looked at me closely. "Then you think he is unusual?"

"Of course. Don't you? And doesn't Miss Gregory?"

"How did you know Miss Gregory thought he was?"

"It was just a feeling I had."

"Well, you're right. She does think so. He's generally been so quiet at home that I didn't really know what she meant until last night. But now . . ." He broke off, still looking at me. "It must have been quite a responsibility."

"You mean Joey?"

"Yes. Feeling that he was unusual. Though I suspect that you would have felt responsible for him anyway."

"I guess so. After all, there are just the two of us."

He nodded. "Yes, I can see that. And it explains a good deal."

"Like what?"

"Well, there are times when I've worried a little

about the two of you, felt you were both a little too good." Then, seeing the look on my face, "I'm sorry. Perhaps I shouldn't have said that."

"It's okay. Only you can't expect me to like it. Only a creep would, because it makes you feel like a hypocrite or a fink. Besides, it's not true. About me, anyway. I get mad and things like everyone else. But at first, when Dad was sick, I didn't want to do anything to upset Mother. And of course I certainly didn't want to afterwards, after Dad died."

"And later on there were your grandparents to be considered."

"That's right. I guess it finally gets to be a habit."

"I guess it does." He smiled. "Possibly a bad habit."

"Maybe. Of course, Joey's different. Because I don't think he ever does get mad, at people or anything else. But if he is too good, it's not in the way you mean."

"What do you mean?"

"Well, the only way he might be too good is for his own good, if you follow me."

"I'm not sure I do."

Once I'd said that much I suppose I could have gone on, told him a lot more. But I decided I'd said enough, for the time being anyway, so I just said, "It doesn't matter. Was there anything else?"

"No. Thanks for telling me everything you have, Mark."

"It's okay," I said again.

He was picking up the phone when I left his study, but I didn't pay any attention to it. On the whole, I wasn't too unhappy at the way our talk had gone. There were things about Joey that I couldn't tell Uncle George because even he wouldn't have believed me. But he was beginning to sense that there was a great deal more to Joey than there seemed to be, and in time maybe I'd be able to talk to him more openly. What I didn't realize was that I was going to *have* to do more talking about Joey—and sooner than I expected.

5

As Joey and I were leaving the house the next morning, I heard Uncle George say something to Aunt Janet about Branford. I knew that Branford was the county seat and that it was about ten miles from Westfield, but I didn't know anything else about it, and I didn't pay any attention to what was being said. I had other things to think about.

Joey wasn't in his room when I came home from school, and at first I thought he was over at Luis'. But when he still wasn't home at five thirty I went downstairs to ask Aunt Janet if she knew where he was, and she said that Uncle George had taken him to Branford after school.

"What for?" I asked. "What's at Branford?"

"The State Teachers College," she said. She looked at me as if she wasn't quite sure how I was going to react. "George knows quite a few people on the staff, and after what happened the other night, he thought it might be a good idea to take Joey there for testing. Intelligence tests, I mean."

Well, that's that, I thought. But all I said was, "I see."

Uncle George and Joey came home rather late, and they were both quiet at supper. There wasn't anything strange about that as far as Joey was concerned, but it was pretty unusual for Uncle George because he usually had quite a lot to say. After supper he asked me to come into his study again.

"I understand your aunt told you where I took Joey this afternoon," he said.

"Yes."

"Do you know what happened?"

"I think so," I said.

"What do you think happened?"

"His score in most tests wasn't just high. It was so high that in some cases they couldn't really measure it."

Uncle George blinked. "How did you know that?"

"Well, you said last night that I probably knew Joey better than anyone else does, and I do. But besides that, they tested him out in Los Angeles, and I heard them talking to Grandpa about it."

"I didn't know that," said Uncle George. "How is it that your grandfather never said anything to me about it?"

"In the first place, I don't think he understood what they meant. I think he just thought they meant that Joey was very bright for his age. And in the second place, it happened right after he and Grandma heard about Aunt Helen's baby, just before we came

East. And he and Grandma were so excited about that, going over to see her, that I guess he forgot."

There was a knock on the front door. Aunt Janet opened it, and I could hear Sally talking to her.

"I don't see how your grandfather could have forgotten anything like that," said Uncle George. "But . . . What do you think we ought to do about it? Joey, I mean."

"Nothing," I said.

"Nothing? I'm afraid *you* don't understand what it means either, Mark. It's terribly important."

"I know it is," I said. "But not in the way you think."

I must have sounded a little impatient because Uncle George looked surprised. But I couldn't help it. There had been many times when I had wished I could talk to someone about Joey, but I didn't feel like it now.

"What do you mean?" asked Uncle George. Then he must have noticed that I was listening to what was going on outside. "That sounds like Sally. Were you going somewhere?"

"Yes. To the movies."

"Oh. Well, I don't want to keep you. But I'd like to go into this a bit more. Let's talk about it again sometime soon."

He came to the door with me. Sally was waiting there with Aunt Janet, and he asked her how her parents were, and then we left. We had a little time before the movie started, so we walked down the hill rather slowly. We talked about the football season that had just started, and Sally wanted to know what I thought about Westfield's chances, and I told her. But at the same time, even though I didn't really want to, I found that I was still thinking about Joey: about what Uncle George had said and what I was going to say when we talked about him again and how I was going to say it. Sally must have noticed because she said, "Is anything wrong, Mark?"

One of the things I liked about Sally was that when she asked something like that I felt she wasn't just being polite. She really wanted to know.

"I'm not sure," I said.

"Does it have anything to do with Joey?"

I looked at her. "What makes you ask that?"

"Well, I know it's not school. You're way ahead of the class in most things. And I don't see how it could be trouble with your uncle and aunt. They're much too nice."

"It does have something to do with Joey," I said, "at least, it might have."

I told her what had happened that afternoon, about how Uncle George had taken Joey up to Branford for testing, and about what he had been saying when Sally arrived.

"But of course Joey's brilliant," she said. "He's probably a genius. But that's not the important thing about him. The important thing is the way he looks at people and things and the way he thinks and feels about them."

I don't know why I was surprised when I had already decided that in a curious way she and Joey were alike. I guess I just wasn't used to having anyone really understand him.

"How do you mean?" I asked.

"Well, there was a boy in high school two years ago, Jimmy Pryor, who was supposed to have a fantastic I.Q. He graduated when he was fifteen, and he won all kinds of scholarships. Of course, I didn't really know him—I was in the sixth grade at the time— but I had a feeling that all he was really interested in was *facts,* what he'd learned in school or from books. But Joey's not like that."

"No," I said. "You're right. He's not. What happened to Jimmy Pryor?"

"Oh, he's at Harvard, doing very well. Even though he was terribly bright he never had any real problems, and I don't think he ever will."

"But you think Joey will."

She hesitated. "He may. There are different ways of being different. People don't mind so much if someone's just smarter than they are. But when someone's *really* different . . ."

"That's what I keep telling him," I said. "He can't help being what he is, and I wouldn't want him to be anything else, but . . . How do you know so much about it?"

She shrugged. "I guess because, in a way, I'm a little different, too. And that's not a good thing to be in a town like this. I had a certain amount of trouble once, but I finally said to myself, 'Everybody doesn't have to know how I think and feel about *everything*. At least, not now. There'll be time enough for that later on.' "

I nodded. It was very much what I'd always thought myself, what I'd been trying to get Joey to see. And once I realized that she not only understood Joey but understood the whole problem, I was tempted to tell her more about him—things I'd never told anyone else. But by that time we had reached the movie theater, and Billy Talbot and a couple of other kids came up and that was that.

The picture was quite good. It was a British mystery, and had me fooled almost to the very end.

It was still fairly early when we got out, and we stood around for a while outside the movie theater. Since it was Friday night, there had been a great many kids from school in the audience. Quite a few of the high school seniors had cars, either the family car or their own jalopy, and they and their girls piled into them and went off just as they had on the night of the band concert.

I said something to Sally about it—that it was too bad there was no place in town we could go to even for a soda—and she said yes. That was something else that Uncle George had been trying to do: set up a youth center or club that would stay open evenings, especially on Friday and Saturday nights.

"That would be great," I said. "Why haven't they done it?"

"Because there are people here who don't think it's necessary. They say that they didn't have anything like it when they were our age, and they don't know why we need it."

"Wally Jordan, for instance?"

"Yes," she said.

I took Sally home, and when I got back to our place, Uncle George and Aunt Janet were still up. They asked me how the movie was, and I told them; then I said goodnight and went upstairs.

Since Joey had been on my mind quite a bit that evening, I looked in at him before I went to bed. His eyes were closed, and he was smiling, not the way he smiles when he's awake, but in a way he does only when he's asleep. I'd seen that particular smile fairly often when we were out in Los Angeles, but it was only the year before that it had come to mean anything to me.

We had been studying the Far East in school—

they were trying out some new social studies ideas on us—and we had been going into how people lived and what they thought in India, China and Japan and, of course, that covered their art. And since a good deal of their art depicted the Buddha, I began doing some reading about him. Joey had been very interested in all this. But for some reason he was specially interested in the *bodhisattvas*, the saints who are said to be born with the Buddha's own spirit in them. If he wants to, a *bodhisattva* can leave the world and attain *nirvana* immediately. But because he cares about people he stays here to help others learn what he's always known: the right way to live.

Then one day I got a book out of the library, and there was a picture of a *bodhisattva* in it, a tenth century Indian bronze. He was seated in the lotus position and he was smiling a small, secret smile—not of amusement, but of understanding. There was something familiar about it, and that night I suddently realized it was the way I'd often seen Joey smile. That started me thinking about him. According to what I'd read, a *bodhisattva* can be born at any time and in any part of the world. And while I would never say anything about it to anyone, and I felt a little silly even to think it, I began wondering whether that wasn't the answer to a lot of things. Because Joey's the only person I've ever known who does smile that way.

I stood there now, looking at Joey and remembering what Sally had said when we were talking about him before. He meant an awful lot to me, more than anyone else in the world, not just because he was my brother and there were just the two of us, but because there had always been this thing between us. I didn't even like to think of not being with him, partly because I knew he needed me and partly because, in a funny way, I knew I needed him. At the same time I knew that, because he was what he was, being close to him was going to mean problems: not just now, but later on too. And I didn't like the idea. I would much rather have kept everything simple, not have to be involved and responsible and all that.

While I was standing there, he opened his eyes and looked at me. I'm not sure he was really awake and knew how mixed up I was about him and everything else, but he kept looking at me. And then suddenly he smiled—not the way he had been smiling, but the way he usually did—and closed his eyes again.

On Monday there was a certain amount of excitement in school. It started early in the morning with some quiet talking among the teachers, and from then on they all seemed to have one eye on the door during classes. While we were having English, Mr. Burton, the principal, came in with a tall, gray-haired man. They sat in the back of the room for about fifteen minutes and then left. I asked Sally who the man with Mr. Burton was, and she said she didn't know. It wasn't the district superintendent—she knew him—but from the way the teachers were acting it might be someone from his office.

During lunch the grey-haired man sat with Mr. Burton, and later on I saw him in the hall talking to Miss Gregory, Joey's teacher. When I got home in the afternoon, there was a car in the driveway, and

Aunt Janet said that Uncle George wanted to see me. I knocked on the door of his study and, when Uncle George told me to come in, there was the gray-haired man again, sitting in the leather chair in the corner.

Uncle George introduced me to him, saying, "This is my nephew, Mark." Then to me, "This is Dr. Dale, head of the psychology department at the State Teachers College."

We shook hands. Uncle George told me to sit down and then said, "Dr. Dale came down from Branford about Joey. He wasn't there Friday when they gave Joey the tests, but he went over them later on and he wanted to find out a little more about Joey."

"His test results were quite astonishing," said Dr. Dale. "And since gifted children are a special interest of mine, I thought I'd like to talk to your uncle, his teacher, and anyone who could give me information about him. Which of course includes you."

"Yes, sir," I said.

"You don't mind?"

"No, sir."

"I understand your father was a physicist."

"Yes, a nuclear physicist. He worked at Los Alamos. That's where Joey was born."

Dr. Dale looked at Uncle George. "Then there could be a hereditary factor involved."

"I suppose so," said Uncle George. "Paul was pretty unusual when he was a boy. And of course he was a brilliant scientist."

"Did he know about Joey, that he was unusual, too?"

"I don't think so. Joey was only two when he died.

And Paul was away a good deal during that last year. In the hospital."

"The hospital?"

"Yes," said Uncle George. He hesitated, looking at me.

"He had radiation poisoning," I said. "There had been an accident in the lab a couple of months before Joey was born. That's what he died of."

"I see," said Dr. Dale. "I'm sorry. I understand that you've known about Joey for some time."

"Yes."

"Your uncle and I have been discussing him. I want to go over his test results again, but I don't ever remember having seen anything like them. Now, as you probably know, the school here isn't exactly the best in the state. But even if it were, it wouldn't be able to do very much for someone like Joey. No regular school can. They're geared to the needs of the average, not the exceptional child. But we do have a special school for gifted children at Branford, and we wondered what you thought about having Joey transferred there."

I didn't answer immediately. I had kind of wanted to talk to Uncle George about Joey, at least in a general way, but I hadn't expected anything like this to come up, and I wasn't sure what to say. Or rather, how to say it.

"We'd really like to know what you think, Mark," said Uncle George finally.

"All right," I said. "I don't think you should do it." It was blunt, but I couldn't think of any other way to put it.

Uncle George and Dr. Dale both looked a little surprised.

"Why do you say that?" asked Uncle George.

I fished for a good way to begin. "Sally and I were talking about Joey last night. She's a girl in my class," I explained to Dr. Dale. "She knows a lot about people, and she knows Joey. I told her about the tests and how surprised Uncle George had been at the results, and she said, 'Of course Joey's brilliant. He may even be a genius. But that's not the important thing about him. The important thing is the way he looks at everything, people and things, and the way he thinks and feels about them.' And she was right."

"What do you mean by that?" asked Dr. Dale. "The way he looks at everything?"

I'd done a good deal of thinking about how I could explain Joey to someone else if I had to. I had never been sure I could. But now I had no choice.

"When we were still out in Los Angeles, they showed a film in school," I began. "It was on psychology, and part of it was on mice and how they learn things. They put the mice in a maze—a large box with lots of passages in it, some of which led some place and some of which didn't. Then they timed the mice to see how long it would take them to get through the maze to the food at the other end."

Dr. Dale nodded.

"Well, while I was watching it I started thinking that maybe most of us are like the mice. I mean, the world's a pretty complicated place to us. We go this way and that, and even if we're very smart, it takes us quite a while to figure out what it's all about and how you get from here to there. But if you could look at the maze in a different way—from above, say, like the psychologists who were running the experiment—it would all seem very simple. You could see the whole pattern, and you could tell exactly which way to go without making a single mistake."

"You mean you think that's the way Joey sees things?" asked Uncle George.

"Yes," I said.

"But how?" asked Dr. Dale. "What makes him able to?"

I'd done some thinking about that, too, wondering whether I could tell anyone about the *bodhisattva* bit, but I decided I couldn't. After all, it was just my own crazy idea. So I said, "I don't know. And I don't know what he's going to do or be when he grows up. I don't think he's going to be a scientist like Dad. I think it's more likely he's going to be a teacher."

"What kind of teacher?" asked Uncle George.

"Not a school teacher or even a college professor, but one of the great teachers," I said. "The kind that everyone in the world can learn from if they'll really listen. The thing is, even if he is terribly intelligent, and of course he is, you can't teach him the really important things even in a special school. He either knows them already, or he'll have to find them out for himself. And one of the things he's going to have to learn is how to get along with other children. Not unusual ones, as intelligent as he is, but average ones. And if he does go to that school in Branford, he won't have a chance to. He'll never be able to make any friends here in Westfield, learn anything about children who aren't unusual."

Uncle George was looking at me thoughtfully. I remembered what he'd said about Dad—how he'd been a little jealous of him when he realized Dad was smarter than he was—and I think he was trying to decide whether I was against Joey's going to the school in Branford because I was jealous of Joey. Then he must have decided that I wasn't and that I'd meant what I said, because he turned to Dr. Dale and said, "He does have a point. That's one of the troubles with schools for gifted children. It does have a way of isolating them, making them seem too special. And that can lead to difficulties later on. So suppose we leave things the way they are for the time being."

I think Dr. Dale may have been a little disappointed, though of course he didn't say so. But I was relieved. Because, for the first time, I had told someone else some of the things I thought about Joey, and they hadn't acted as if I were out of my mind. They, Uncle George in particular, seemed to understand and accept it.

6

LATE THE NEXT AFTERNOON UNCLE GEORGE HAD another visitor, Wally Jordan. Uncle George had made some new kitchen shelves for Aunt Janet, and I was helping him put them up when a car stopped outside. There were footsteps on the porch, the front door opened, and Wally Jordan came in—as usual without knocking. He nodded to Aunt Janet and said, "If you've got a minute, I want to talk to you, George."

"All right, Wally," said Uncle George. "Do you want to measure that shelf again, Mark? I think it's a little big."

He and Wally Jordan went into the study and I started checking the length of the shelf. But since Uncle George hadn't closed the door, Aunt Janet and I could hear everything that was said.

"Exactly what are you up to, George?" asked Jordan.

"What do you mean, Wally?"

" I understand that one of your pals from the State Teachers College was down here yesterday, spent the day at the school."

"If you mean Dr. Dale, I don't know that I'd call him a pal. As a matter of fact, I had never met him before yesterday."

"He came here afterwards, spent at least an hour talking to you."

"That's right."

"About what?"

"As it happens, about a personal matter."

"Personal?"

"Yes. We were talking about my nephew Joey."

"You mean how he's practically a genius, something like that?"

"Something like that."

"Do you expect me to believe that?"

"That Joey's an unusual boy?"

"No. About why that Dr. Dale was here. I asked you what you were up to, but I know what you're up to. You're worried about what's going to happen to that report of yours, what the school board is going to do about it, aren't you?"

"It's not my report, Wally. Almost everyone in the PTA worked on it, made suggestions. All I did was write the final draft."

"But you're the one who's been pushing it. And because you're worried, you called in some long-haired professor to back you up on it."

"I told you why Dr. Dale came down here. Because of Joey. Before he talked to me, he talked to

Miss Gregory. But while he was at the school he *did* look around a bit. And I can tell you that he wasn't too impressed with what he saw."

"So what? What's he got to do with it?"

"He happens to be an educator, and a very good one."

"What difference does that make? I'm not interested in what he thinks or what anyone thinks."

"What are you interested in, Wally?"

Wally Jordan's voice had been getting louder and louder. Uncle George's was as quiet as ever, but there was something in it that I hadn't heard before. I looked at Aunt Janet, and I could tell that she had heard it, too.

"I'm interested in the same thing I've been interested in for the last ten years, all the time I've been in office," said Wally Jordan. "I'm interested in keeping things the way they are! Where do you think we'd get the money for the school budget you're proposing?"

"If you'd read the report carefully you'd know. Most of the additional money would come from state and federal aid."

"And have a lot of outsiders coming in here and telling us what to do? Not while I'm First Selectman!"

"Then maybe it's time we had a different First Selectman."

"What did you say?"

"I said then maybe it's time we had a different First Selectman."

"So that's it! That's what you're really after! You want to be First Selectman yourself!"

"No, I don't, Wally."

"Not much! Just the way you didn't want to get involved in the PTA. All right, George. Now I know where we stand."

I caught a glimpse of him as he came storming out of the study, and I heard the front door slam behind him. A moment later Uncle George came into the kitchen. He didn't say anything, and neither did Aunt Janet. They just looked at one another. Then Aunt Janet smiled a kind of funny little smile and it suddently dawned on me that Joey and I weren't the only ones who could tell what the other was thinking. Aunt Janet knew that Uncle George had made up his mind about something and, although she was a little worried about it, she was glad, too.

Later on, it occurred to me that if Wally Jordan knew about Joey and the tests, then a lot of other people must know about it, too, especially at school. I couldn't help but wonder how they felt about it. Well, I found out the next afternoon.

Billy Talbot and I were hacking around on the football field. We were practising passing from center, and as Billy told me later, I had just whipped one back that caught him on the tip of the finger. He had not only dropped the ball, but it had hurt. And that may have been why he suddenly said, "Here he comes."

"Who?" I asked, picking up the ball.

"Go-go Joey."

I turned around. Sure enough, Joey was standing a short distance away on the edge of the field. I turned back to Billy.

"What do you mean, go-go Joey?"

"Why, everybody knows he's the big brain around here, the gee whiz quiz kid."

Billy was probably the best friend I had in Westfield, but when I get mad I'm afraid I don't think about things like that. And I was good and mad now.

"Cut it out!" I said shoving him in the chest.

"Don't tell me what to do and what not to do!" he said, shoving me back.

"I will when it comes to Joey," I said. "Lay off him."

"Make me!"

"Okay!" And I shoved him again, hard.

He staggered back a few steps then, angry, too, he really came at me. Billy's a bit heavier than I am, but I got hold of his sleeve, pivoted and gave him the old hip throw. Only, instead of slamming him down hard, I held on to him and eased him on to his back.

"Hey!" he said.

I left him there. Joey was walking away, and I went after him.

"Where are you going?" I asked.

"Home," he said.

"What are you so upset about?"

He didn't answer, but I knew. He didn't like any kind of violence. Now I got angry at him. I'd had enough, more than enough. After all, it was because of him that I'd had the run-in with Billy.

"Look," I said, "I'm not you. I get mad about things. If you don't like it then why do you keep making it so tough for me? Why don't you start acting a little more like everyone else?"

83

He stared at me, his eyes very large, then he went on again up the street. By this time Billy was on his feet, and he came over to me.

"Man, you really put me down," he said. "Where'd you learn how to do that?"

"In Los Angeles. I had a friend whose father taught self-defense."

"That's what I figured." Then, "I'm sorry I said what I did. About Joey, I mean. I don't know why I said it, because I like him. I'm not sure I get him, but I like him."

"It's all right," I said.

"Sure?"

"Yes."

He held out his hand, and I took it; but we both felt a little funny about what had happened, and after a few more passes, we called it a day.

Joey was still in sight as I started home, but I didn't hurry to catch up with him. And watching him walk up the street, past all the white houses with their lawns and porches, I suddenly realized why Sally had always seemed to have some reservations about Westfield. One of the reasons I had liked it was that it was such a picture post card, Currier and Ives sort of town.

Everything belonged, even the stores with their Colonial fronts. But now I saw that it wasn't exactly an ideal place for someone who didn't belong, someone like Joey. It wouldn't have mattered in Los Angeles or New York. They were so big that no one stands out. But it mattered here. People were beginning to notice him because they sensed that he was

different. And if they ever realized just how different he really was, they wouldn't just notice him. He'd be as conspicuous as a delegation of Tibetan monks looking for the latest incarnation of the Dalai Lama in the A&P.

When I came down for breakfast the next morning, Joey had already finished his. He was sitting at the kitchen table watching Aunt Janet make sandwiches.

"Good morning," I said. I looked at the sandwiches. "Someone going on a picnic?"

"In a way," said Aunt Janet. "Joey's class is going on a trip, and your uncle's going with them. They'll be gone most of the day, so I'm fixing lunch for them."

"Where are you going?" I asked Joey.

"To see a power plant and visit some Indians."

"Indians?" I glanced at Aunt Janet.

She nodded. "There's a small colony of Scatacooks about five miles up the river. They do some farming, make baskets, brooms, things like that, and every year the first grade goes up there to visit them."

"What about the power plant?"

"There's a hydroelectric plant about a mile from there, so George always goes along to take the children through that and explain how it works."

"Sounds like fun," I said. "You'll have to tell me about it when you get back, Joey."

He nodded. He'd been rather quiet last night, but now his eyes were bright, and it was obvious that he was looking forward to the trip. Aunt Janet gave him his sandwiches and a thermos of milk, and we went outside to wait for Sally.

About ten o'clock I heard one of the school buses leaving, but we were just starting English and I didn't pay any attention to it, didn't think about the trip again until late in the afternoon.

I had gym that day so I didn't leave school until almost four. I was starting across the Green with Billy Talbot to have a coke at the drugstore, when the bus that had taken Joey's class on the trip came up the street. Uncle George was the first one out, and somehow I knew something was wrong even before I saw his face. I told Billy to go ahead, that I'd be along later, and I went over to the bus.

"What is it, Uncle George?" I asked. "What happened?"

"Eddie Jordan's lost," he said.

"Lost?"

"When we got back to where we'd left the bus, we let the kids play for a while. And when we were about to leave, we discovered that he wasn't around. We called, looked for him, but we couldn't find him."

Since it was Eddie Jordan, I didn't feel quite the same about it as if it were one of the other kids. But even though I didn't like him, getting lost couldn't be any fun. Besides, Uncle George was involved.

"What are you going to do?"

"Call his father and the police and go back there again."

"Can I come with you?" I asked.

He hesitated. "All right. We'll probably need all the help we can get. My car's in the parking lot. I'll meet you there."

He went into the school, and I stood there for a minute or two, watching the children get off the bus. They were all quiet, but they didn't look too upset. I guess Miss Gregory and Uncle George had told them there was nothing to be worried about. Joey and Miss Gregory were the last ones off. Miss Gregory was quite pale.

"Did your uncle tell you?" she asked.

"Yes."

"I can't understand it. It's never happened before. We called and called and looked everywhere. Of course, there were only three of us—your uncle, the bus driver and I—and I had to stay with the other children. We were afraid to let them help look, too, because of the river and the woods."

"I'm going back there with Uncle George," I said. "I'm sure we'll find him."

"You won't have too much time," she said. "We're going to have a storm."

I looked to the west. Dark, heavy clouds were moving in over the hills.

"It'll be quite a while before it gets here," I said.

"It will get there, to where he was lost, before it gets here," she said. "I'd better go in, see if there's anything I can do."

She went into the school, and I turned to see Joey still standing there, looking at me.

"I don't know," I said. "We'll have to see what Uncle George says." Then, "All right. Come on."

We went around to the back of the school where the teachers parked their cars. A few minutes later Uncle George came up.

"What are you doing here, Joey?" he asked.

"He wants to come with us," I said. "He thinks he knows which way Eddie went."

"Which way was that?"

"Down towards the river," said Joey.

"I'm not sure it's a good idea for you to come," said Uncle George. "You know what it's like there. It's pretty wild."

"I know. But I'll be careful. Please, Uncle George."

He hesitated again. "All right," he said finally.

A patrol car with two of the town policemen in it turned into the parking lot, and Uncle George went over to talk to them. While they were talking, a station wagon drove up and stopped nearby. Wally Jordan was driving and Fred Jordan, Eddie's father, sat next to him. Neither of them got out or said anything, but from the way they looked at Uncle George it was clear what they were thinking: that what had happened was his fault. And of course if he couldn't even handle a first grade trip, who would trust him with anything important? Why should anyone accept his recommendations on the school budget, for instance, or listen to any of his ideas on things he wanted to do for the school and the town?

7

THE STATION WAGON FOLLOWED US AS UNCLE
George drove out of the parking lot, and the patrol
car with the two police followed the station wagon.
We went around the Green, down past the railroad
station and across the bridge. We started north on
the highway on the other side of the river, but after
we had gone two or three miles, we turned off on to
a dirt road that led us back towards the river again.
We were in the shadow of the hills there, but even
then it seemed much darker than it should have. I
looked up and saw that Miss Gregory had been right.
The storm clouds were almost overhead. The air
was heavy, oppressive, and somehow the fact that a
storm was coming up made it all the more exciting,
even more of an adventure.

We drove along the dirt road for about a mile.
There were woods on both sides of the road, and
while we could hear the river in the distance, we

couldn't see it. Then we came to a large clearing—a recreation area with a stone fireplace and a few tables and benches. Uncle George pulled in near the fireplace and stopped. There was another car there with two state troopers in it. Uncle George got out of the car and went over to talk to them, and Wally and Fred Jordan and the two policemen joined them. Then Fred and Wally Jordan and Uncle George came back to where Joey and I were waiting. Eddie's father was thinner than Wally Jordan and the few times I had seen him before he had always looked a little worried. He looked more worried than ever now.

"Your uncle says you think you know which way Eddie went," he said to Joey.

"Yes," said Joey. "Down toward the river."

"Will you show us exactly where?"

"Yes," said Joey.

"Just a second," said Wally Jordan. He waved to the police and the troopers, and they nodded—the police going towards the woods north of the clearing and the troopers towards the south.

"All right," said Jordan. "Go ahead."

Joey led the way across the clearing and down the bank to the river. It was fairly narrow there and didn't seem to be too deep. Joey went upstream to the narrowest point where there was a large, flat rock. There were other rocks beyond it like natural stepping stones. Joey went out on the flat rock.

"You mean he went across here?" said Wally Jordan.

"Yes," said Joey.

"Did you see him go over?"

"No," said Joey.

"Then how do you know he did?"

"I just know it."

"That's ridiculous!" said Jordan.

"Seems to me it's worth a try," said Uncle George. "But you don't have to come with us. Why don't you stay here with the troopers and the police, and I'll go over with the boys?"

Jordan looked at the woods on the other side of the river, then at Eddie's father.

"No," he said. "We'll come too."

Joey jumped from the flat rock to the one next to it and made his way across. Uncle George and I followed him and Wally Jordan and Eddie's father followed us. It was even easier than it had looked.

The woods seemed wilder across the river, more untouched, than on the other side. But Joey started off through the trees without hesitation, going upstream and slightly inland, away from the river.

Grandfather had been a great one for picnics and camping trips so I'd been out in some fairly rough country with Joey before this. He had always liked it, been very interested in everything there was to see. But now he seemed, not just interested, but intent. He moved like an Indian, quietly, picking his way through the underbrush and looking around in all directions. At first I thought he was following a trail or footprints, and he may have been. But then we came out into a small clearing, and he paused, looking up into a huge oak. I looked up also and there was a squirrel clinging to the trunk, head down, just above the first branch.

Joey and the squirrel stared at each other for a moment. Then, with a flirt of its tail, the squirrel circled around the tree trunk and disappeared. As it did, Joey went on again, but now he bore more to the right, moving farther away from the river. I'm not sure anyone else noticed because at that moment there was a rumble of thunder in the distance and Uncle George and the two Jordans turned to look up at the dark and threatening sky.

"Where are you going now?" asked Wally Jordan. Joey pointed.

"That's crazy!" said Jordan. "Even if he did come over here he wouldn't head off into the woods like that."

"He may have lost his way," said Uncle George. "But let's not have an argument every couple of minutes. If you don't think he came in here, why don't you two cut back to the river?"

Again Jordan hesitated. "Eddie!" he shouted. "Eddie!"

There was silence except for the rustling of the leaves, the distant sound of the river.

"What do you think?" Jordan asked Eddie's father. I don't know what the answer was, but as Uncle George and I followed Joey across the clearing, the two men came after us.

We went on again, Joey leading the way and constantly looking around him. He stopped twice after that. The first time was when a blue jay flew toward us, calling loudly. It circled overhead, then went off toward the river. The next time was when we were in some fairly thick cover. Joey stood there for a moment, staring at a clump of birches, and I wasn't sure what he was looking at. Then I saw a faint movement in the underbrush and I realized a hen pheasant was hidden there and was watching Joey just as the squirrel had done. Both times, after he had stopped, Joey went on again in a slightly different direction—almost as if he had been told which way to go.

We were approaching the base of a hill now, and the ground was rising and becoming rocky.

"George!" called Wally Jordan from behind us. "Hold up! I said this was crazy and it is!"

He was interrupted by another rumble of thunder, closer this time. Then, as he came towards us impatiently, Joey stopped again. A huge slab of rock leaned against the side of the hill, making a shallow cave. And huddled just inside it, looking very small, was Eddie Jordan.

Joey looked at him and he looked at Joey, and in that moment—because Joey knew—I also knew what had happened. Eddie had crossed the river and gone into the woods in order to hide and scare Uncle George. And, having gone farther than he had intended, he had lost his way and ended up here.

"Eddie!" said his father. He hurried forward and picked him up, and as he did Eddie burst into tears.

"Are you all right?" asked Wally Jordan. Still crying, Eddie nodded. But instead of being relieved, Jordan seemed angry.

"How did you know where he was?" he asked Joey.

"I just did," said Joey.

"What do you mean, you just did?" said Jordan. "There's only one way you could know it. If you took him across the river, got him lost, and then left him here!"

"Don't be silly, Wally," said Uncle George. "Joey would never do anything like that."

"No?"

"No," said Uncle George. Then, as thunder rumbled again and lightning flashed, "Come on. Let's get back to the cars before we get soaked."

Fred Jordan, still carrying Eddie, had already started back the way we had come, and Uncle George and Joey followed them. But Wally Jordan stood there stubbornly.

"Can you think of any other way he could have found him like that?" he asked me.

As a matter of fact, I could. Apparently Jordan hadn't seen Joey studying the squirrel, the jay, and the pheasant. And although I didn't think they had actually *talked* to Joey, told him which way Eddie had gone, I had a feeling that because he had really looked at them—seen them, as he saw everything, in his own particular way—he may have understood them just as a grown-up can understand what a baby means or wants before it can speak. But of course I couldn't say that.

"Yes," I said.

"How?"

"Well, he could have thought, 'If I were Eddie, where would I go? Which way?' And when he went there, there Eddie was."

It was a good try, but it wasn't good enough. If

anything, it made Wally Jordan even angrier.

"What are you trying to say—that he's a mind-reader or something? There's only one way he could have known—the way I said!"

There was another rumble of thunder, louder and closer than before. But it wasn't loud enough to bring me to my senses because now I was getting mad, really mad. It was bad enough for Wally Jordan to be always going after Uncle George. But now he was going after Joey too, practically calling him a liar and a sneak when, if anyone was, it was Eddie.

"Didn't you hear what Uncle George said?"

"That your smart alec brother wouldn't do anything like that? Yes, I heard him."

"But you didn't believe him! Can't you get it through your head that Joey isn't just bright? He's special! There isn't anything, practically anything, he couldn't do if he really wanted to."

"What do you mean, there isn't anything he couldn't do?"

"Well, there isn't!" I said, still angry. "Practically anything! If he wanted to, I'll bet . . ." A blue jay flew by, possibly the same one we'd seen before. "Well, I'll bet he could even fly!"

"What?"

"I'll bet he could!" I said.

Then, as the rain started coming down, pattering more and more loudly on the leaves overhead, I turned and began running back down through the woods.

I caught up with Uncle George and Joey just as they reached the river. Fred Jordan, still carrying

Eddie, was just crossing the stepping stones, and we crossed after him. By the time we reached the car, it was raining hard.

We sat there in the car for several minutes, waiting for Wally Jordan. When he appeared, he was walking slowly in spite of the rain, as if he was thinking about something. He got into the station wagon, and Uncle George started the car and we went back along the road to town.

We were all quiet during the drive home. Joey's eyes were closed, and he seemed to be asleep. I looked back once or twice and saw that one of the other cars was following us but, because of the rain, I couldn't tell whether it was Wally Jordan's station wagon or the police car.

It was still raining when we got to the house. Uncle George took a blanket from the back seat, threw it over Joey's shoulders and ran inside with him. I was about to go in, too, when the car that had been following us pulled into the driveway. Now I could see that it was the station wagon. The door opened, and Wally Jordan got out and came over.

"I've been thinking about what you said back there in the woods," he said. "About Joey and what he can do. You were kidding of course."

I was still angry at what he'd said—acting as if it was Joey's fault that Eddie had gotten lost—so angry that I said, "No. I wasn't kidding."

"Well, if he really is that special, there are a couple of people who should know about it. Do you think he'd be willing to kind of show us sometime?"

He was being very quiet about it, and I wasn't sure

I liked it.

"What for?" I asked. "Why should he?"

"In other words, you were lying about that and about him and Eddie . . ."

"No, I wasn't! Okay. I guess maybe he'd be willing to show you."

"Fine," he said. "I'll get in touch with you."

8

AUNT JANET WAS WAITING FOR ME WHEN I WENT inside. She had already sent Joey upstairs to take a hot bath and change his clothes and, since I was just as wet as he was, she made me go up to bathe and change, too.

When we came down again, supper was ready. Uncle George must have told Aunt Janet what had happened: how Joey had found Eddie. And though she didn't say anything about it, I could tell how she felt about it—and about Joey—from the way she kept looking at him.

A long letter had come from Grandpa and Grandma that afternoon, and after supper Uncle George read it to us. It wasn't just about Aunt Helen and her baby; her first, which was why it was so important. It was about London, too: Buckingham Palace and the Tower and the parks and the people. And even though Grandpa had some things to say about the traffic, which he claimed was as bad as it was in Los Angeles and all going the wrong way, you could tell he was really enjoying himself.

I had some homework to do, and after we had talked about the letter for a while, I excused myself and went upstairs. I had to write a paper for English, and it was only when I finished it that I began to think about it all: what had happened that afternoon and what I'd said. And then, for the first time, I began to realize what it meant, and I wasn't at all happy about it.

I was still sitting at my desk when Joey came upstairs. The door between our rooms was open, as it usually was, and he must have known that something was wrong almost immediately because he came to the door and stood there. I looked at him, but I didn't say anything until he said, "What is it, Mark?"

"Nothing," I said, trying to keep the whole thing out of my mind. Then, when he continued to stand there, looking a little hurt, "All right. It's Wally Jordan. You remember what he said about you and Eddie? That the only way you could have found him like that was if you had taken him into the woods and gotten him lost?" Joey nodded. "Well, after you and Uncle George started back, he kept on about it, and I got mad and told him that finding Eddie was nothing. That you could do practically anything if you really wanted to."

He didn't ask what I'd meant by practically anything, but he didn't have to because, of course, he could tell what I was thinking—how stupid I'd been to say what I had. And, even worse, to say he'd show

strange expression on his face. It was like the expression you see on a kid's face when you first show him the old hand trick: the one where you get him to put his crossed hands palm to palm and interlock the fingers, then tell him to move this finger or that one. It's an expression that says: these are my hands so I know I can do it; it's just a question of figuring out which finger is which.

Then, as I watched, Joey's expression cleared and slowly, very slowly, he rose up into the air and floated a few feet over the bed. He remained there for a minute or two, floating in mid-air and smiling a little, looking completely relaxed. Then, just as slowly, he sank down on to the bed again. One of the reasons I think I must have dreamed it is that I wasn't at all surprised. It was as if I had known Joey could do it if he really wanted to, just as I had said. Smiling a little, also, I closed my eyes and went back to sleep.

I didn't exactly forget what happened that night or what I thought had happened—just as I didn't forget what I'd said to Wally Jordan or what he had said to me. But I didn't say anything to Joey about it, maybe because I was afraid of what *he'd* say, and after a while I stopped thinking about it. I guess what I was hoping was that Wally Jordan really *would* forget about it and that would be the end of it.

Nothing out of the ordinary happened for a couple of days, and I began to breathe easier. But then one afternoon as I went up the hall after my last class, I had the feeling that quite a few people were looking at me, mostly teachers and high school juniors and seniors. I was at my locker getting some books I wanted to take back to the library when I heard someone come up behind me. I turned. It was Wally Jordan.

"I've been looking for you," he said. "You remember what you said about your brother?"

I tried to stall.

"I said a lot of things."

"That's right. What I'm talking about it your saying he'd be willing to show us how special he is. Well, how about having him do it this afternoon?"

"This afternoon?"

"Yeah. I've set it all up, arranged to have a few people come in. Have him here at the school at four thirty." And without giving me a chance to say anything, he went off down the hall.

I stood there for a moment feeling numb. Then I did what I should have done in the first place: I went to talk to Uncle George about it. He wasn't in his room, so I went to the science lab and he wasn't there either, but Miss Lawlor, the assistant science teacher, was.

"Your uncle?" she said. "Why, he left a few minutes after three, went up to Branford."

"What for?" I asked.

"A county PTA meeting. He's the school representative." Then, looking at me, "Is anything wrong?"

"No," I said. "Nothing."

It was then that I realized how I'd underestimated Wally Jordan. He had known about the PTA meeting, known that Uncle George would be going, and had waited until he left before he told me about the arrangements that he'd made. I decided to forget about the library and go home. I couldn't talk to Uncle George, but I could talk to Aunt Janet.

The house was strangely quiet, and at first I thought that Aunt Janet was out in the garden. But when I went into the kitchen there, in the center of the table, was a note.

"Gone to Branford with your uncle to do some shopping," it said. "Cookies in the cookie jar and milk in the refrigerator. Back about six. Love, Aunt J."

I put the note back on the table, went outside and sat down on the porch. A few minutes later Joey came up the street. I don't know what he was thinking about, but he was smiling a little and watching where he walked, being careful not to step on any of the cracks in the sidewalk. And when he came to a tricky place where he had to do a skip-step and almost lost his balance, he didn't look at all different, special or unusual. He looked like any other boy his age on his way home from school.

He didn't see me till he came in the gate. But the minute he did see me, he knew. He paled and his eyes became very large.

"What time?" he asked.

"Four thirty," I said.

"Where?"

"The school. Look, Joey, you don't have to do it. I can still . . ."

"No," he said. "I'll do it."

He went into the house and up the stairs to his room. He didn't say anything, but I knew he wanted to be alone, so I didn't go up after him. I stayed there on the porch, and I had never felt lonelier in my life.

About twenty after four Joey came downstairs. He was still pale, but he looked calm—the way you look when you're going in to an exam that you know is going to be tough, but that you've prepared for as well as you can. Again he didn't say anything, and I didn't either. I got up, and we went off down the street towards the school.

There were quite a few cars parked in front of the school, and I could hear voices and the sound of a football being kicked on the field out in back, but there were no signs of anything in particular going on in the building itself. Wally Jordan was waiting just inside the door.

"This way," he said.

I'm not sure where I had thought he was going to take us—possibly to one of the offices or perhaps a classroom since he had talked about a few people who would be interested. But again I had misjudged him. He led the way to the school auditorium and opened the door of the small room that was just behind the stage, the room where speakers waited before they came out to address the school.

"Wait here," he said.

Joey and I went in, and he closed the door behind us. There were two old chairs in the room and a rickety table. Joey sat down on one of the chairs, but I didn't sit down. I went over to the other door, the one that led to the stage, opened it a crack and looked out.

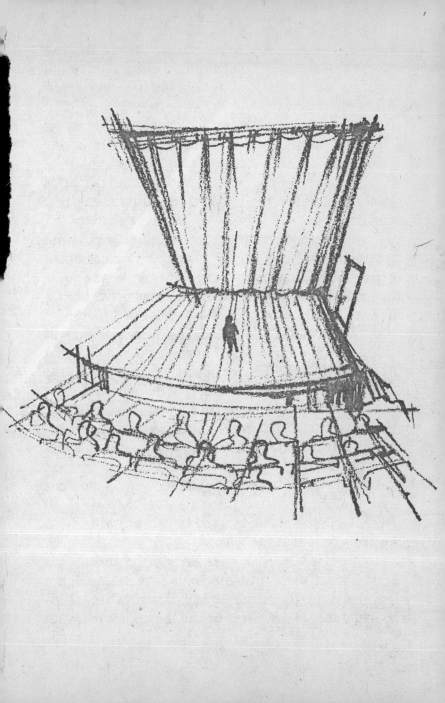

I had been numb, dazed, before. Now I felt sick. Because the auditorium was almost full. In the first few rows were at least a dozen of the most important people in Westfield: Mr. Jessup, the bank president; Mr. Grant, who owned the department store; Mr. Fabian, the real estate man, Mr. Blaine, the attorney; the other two selectmen; and the members of the school board. Behind them sat Mr. Burton, the principal, and most of the teachers. And behind them was at least half the high school, mostly juniors and seniors.

I shut the door, turned and looked at Joey. Until that moment I don't think I was really clear about what Wally Jordan was doing and why he was doing it. I thought that even though he may have been a little annoyed at Joey because of what had happened with Eddie at the house and in the woods he was still somewhat interested in him. Now I realized that he wasn't interested in Joey at all. At least, not in the fact that he was unusual. Because he didn't think he was. What he was interested in was in showing up Uncle George. And since Uncle George clearly believed in Joey or he wouldn't have taken him to Branford for those tests, if Jordan could make Joey look foolish, it would make Uncle George and all his ideas look foolish, too—and that would be the end of all Uncle George's plans, everything he was trying to do for the school and the town.

Joey stared back at me. Though he must have known what was waiting for him in there, he didn't look nervous. But since he had closed his mind, as he had done several times before, I couldn't tell what he was thinking or how he felt. I knew how I felt though. There was no one in the world who knew Joey as well as I did. Therefore, no one else knew how much was at stake. Something had to be done about what was happening. And, since I was the only one there who not only knew but cared, it was up to me to do it. The trouble was, I didn't know what to do.

9

I CONTINUED STANDING THERE FOR A MOMENT. IT
was clear that Jordan—and the audience—was waiting for someone or something. Though the auditorium was quiet, I could sense the presence of
everyone who was in there, and I knew that Joey
could, too. But while I felt weak in the knees, as if
I were the one who was going to have to go out there,
Joey looked completely calm, as if it had nothing to
do with him.

Suddenly the hall door opened and there was Uncle
George. His face was drawn, but he was doing his
best to appear undisturbed. Dr. Dale was with him.
My heart skipped a beat. I was no longer completely
alone.

"Hello, boys," said Uncle George.

I nodded, unable to speak.

"Can I talk to you for a minute, Mark?" asked
Uncle George. "Out here?"

Again I nodded. I went out into the hall, closing the door behind me.

"How did you know?" I asked Uncle George. "What made you come back?"

"I brought him," said Dr. Dale. "Wally Jordan called me and told me if I was interested in Joey I should be here at four thirty. I wasn't sure what he meant, but I decided I ought to talk to your uncle about it. I got hold of him at the PTA meeting, and we came down together."

"Is that what Jordan's waiting for now?" I asked. "You?"

"I suppose so," said Dr. Dale.

So that was it. When Jordan showed Joey up, made him look ridiculous, he wanted Dr. Dale to be there, too, because he wanted him—as well as everyone else—to think that the tests had been an accident and that they didn't mean anything.

"Exactly what's going on?" asked Uncle George. "Do you know?"

"I think so," I said. I told him what I'd said to Wally Jordan in the woods and afterwards, when we got back to the house.

"But why?" asked Uncle George. "Why did you agree to let Joey make a spectacle of himself?"

"I didn't want to," I said, "but it kind of got away from me. At first I was angry at Jordan for saying what he did about Joey, his not realizing that Joey wasn't like anyone else. And later, when he told me that he'd made the arrangements for this afternoon . . . Well, it's not easy to say no to someone like him. And besides, he didn't give me a chance."

"No, he wouldn't," he said. "Well, luckily I got here in time. I'll go in and put a stop to this whole thing right now."

"No, Uncle George," I said. "You can't."

"Why not?"

"Don't you realize that Jordan did all this because of you? Because he's worried about you and your ideas? If you go in and stop this, it will make you look like a phoney. As if you don't really believe in Joey or in those tests yourself. And then what chance will you have of getting any of the things you've been fighting for?"

"If you're talking about the new school budget," he said, "do you think I care about that? I mean, of course I care about it, but we'll battle that out with Wally Jordan at the next town meeting. Or, if we have to, at the next election. The important thing right now is Joey."

"That's right," I said. "But . . ."

"Just a minute, Mark," said Dr. Dale. "Do you remember what you said when your uncle and I wanted Joey to go to our school in Branford? You were against it because you felt it would make him seem too special and that would cut him off from everyone his own age. Well, don't you see how this would be even worse? Obviously you didn't mean what you said about his being able to fly,"—he didn't give me a chance to say that I did mean it, though I probably wouldn't have—"but the fact is that he's not merely gifted. He's apparently a good deal more than that. And if he stood up there and gave a public demonstration of some of the things he's capable of . . ."

"I know," I said. "That's what I've been thinking about, too."

And I had been. I had been thinking, not just about what it would be like for Joey not to have any friends, not to learn how other people think, but about something else. I had been wondering what it would do to him at his age or even a few years from now to have everyone constantly watching him, waiting for him to say or do something remarkable. After all, Siddhartha, who became the Buddha, had been almost thirty when he left his home to look for enlightenment, and almost forty when he sat under the Bo tree.

"Then you can see why I've got to go in there," said Uncle George.

"No," I said. "It's too late for that. Too many people know about that already—about those tests— practically everyone in the school."

"I'm afraid that was my fault," said Dr. Dale. "When I came down here, I had to tell Miss Gregory why I was so interested in Joey."

"It's not just your fault," said Uncle George. "It's mine, too. I didn't really think it through. The thing is, we've got to do something about it, and . . ."

"I'd like to ask you something," I said. "Do you believe what I told you about Joey? Not just about what he's like and why, but about what he can be some day?"

Uncle George and Dr. Dale glanced at one another, then they both nodded.

"Yes," said Uncle George.

"All right," I said. "Then let me handle it."

"How?" asked Uncle George.

"I'd like to talk to him."

"Will it take very long?" asked Dr. Dale. "Jordan knows I'm here. He's waiting for me to come in . . ."

"No," I said. "It won't take long."

I went back into the small room. Joey was sitting where I'd left him, and he looked at me.

"Uncle George doesn't think you should do it," I said. "Go out there, I mean."

"Why not?"

"He just doesn't think you should."

He went on looking at me and while I wasn't sure I could do what he had done so often lately, close my mind to him, I tried to think about what I was saying and nothing else. A strange expression came over his face, an expression I'd never seen before, part sullen and part stubborn.

"Stop that," I said. "I've told you a dozen times not to do that, just think things. Why can't you say them like everyone else?"

"All right," he said. "I don't care."

"What do you mean, you don't care?"

"I don't care what Uncle George says. I'm going out there anyway."

"Why?"

"Because I want to. I don't like Mr. Jordan. He thinks he knows a lot, but he doesn't know anything. I'm going to show him."

"Show him what?"

"You'll see."

"I'll bet!" I was suddenly furious. I realized later

it was myself I was angry with, but I didn't know it then, and it was a good thing I didn't know it because it helped me to say what I had to say. "This is what you've been waiting for, isn't it? A chance to really show off, show everyone just how wonderful you are! What are you going to do—answer all his questions, read his mind and then end up flying around the auditorium?"

His face white and his eyes enormous, he nodded.

"Well, of all the dopey and conceited little creeps! Who do you think you are—Superman, Batman . . . or maybe a *bodhisattva?* Do you want to know what you really are? You're just a stupid kid with a lot of crazy ideas in his head about how great he is!"

He stared at me, stricken, and his expression now was much the same as it had been when the nurse came out of the hospital room, and we knew that mother was dead. Only he had had me then. Now he had no one.

The other door—the door to the auditorium—opened.

"All right, Joey," said Jordan. "We're ready. Come on."

Joey didn't move.

"I said, come on!"

Slowly, as if he were walking in his sleep, Joey got up and followed Jordan out on to the stage.

10

THE DOOR CLOSED BEHIND THEM, AND I STOOD there feeling not the way Joey must have felt, but worse, much worse. Because while Joey may have felt abandoned, betrayed by the person he loved most in the world, he could not have felt guilty. But I did. Though I had done what I did for what seemed like good reasons, I had been not merely brutal, but vicious. I had not only ridiculed him, the brother who meant so much to me, I had mocked his ideas and acted as if I had never believed in them or in him.

Through the closed door I could hear Jordan's voice. He was introducing Joey, saying that everyone there either knew him or knew about him, had heard how unusual he was, and that this was a very special occasion because Joey had agreed to give a public demonstration of some of his extraordinary abilities. He suggested that they begin with some calculations that Joey would do in his head, and he gave him a number with six digits to be multiplied by a number with five digits.

Silence. Alone in the small anteroom and staring at the closed door, I still seemed to see what was taking place out there in the auditorium: Joey looking small and lost on the stage, standing there with his eyes wide and fixed on Jordan—not moving and not answering.

Perhaps that was too difficult a problem, said Jordan. After all, those were pretty big numbers. What about these? And he gave him another pair, both in the hundreds.

Still no word from Joey.

Had he hit one of Joey's weak spots? Jordan sounded almost apologetic. When he was Joey's age, they hadn't had any fancy tests that could tell whether you were a genius or not, but they did expect you to know the three *R*'s. He wouldn't ask Joey how much two and two was, but perhaps Joey would care to tell those assembled there what had happened in 1492?

Again silence, not a word from Joey, but there was the beginning of a stir, the faintest of murmurs from the audience.

But perhaps that was unfair, too, said Jordan. He had only heard indirectly about Joey's intellectual capabilities. What they were really there for was a really special exhibition. For this unusual youngster, who could do anything if he really wanted to, would now prove how unusual he was by doing something that no one outside of a comic strip had ever done before. He would fly!

I'm not sure who started the laughter. It was probably one of the younger girls, and it must have been at least partly the result of nerves, tension. But it triggered a reaction, set off a wave that mounted and spread until it filled the auditorium. As before, though the door was closed, I still saw Joey standing there white-faced, buffeted by the storm of laughter. Then, as it reached its peak—

"Stop that!" said Uncle George. "Stop it, all of you!"

I don't know where he was when he said it, possibly the rear of the auditorium, but there was something in his voice that cut through the laughter like the crack of a whip, cut through it and stopped it instantly. In the quiet that followed I could hear his footsteps as he walked down the aisle and mounted the steps to the stage.

"All right, Joey," he said gently. "Come on."

The door opened, and he stood there for a moment with one hand on Joey's shoulder.

"Wait in there with Mark," he said. "I won't be long."

He shut the door again, went back out on to the stage. I had caught just a glimpse of Jordan standing there, looking startled and somewhat shamefaced.

"You've been in office for a long time, Wally," said Uncle George quietly, almost conversationally. "And like anyone in politics you've probably done some things you were proud of and some things you were ashamed of. But I don't think you or anyone else has ever done anything as despicable as what you did here this afternoon."

I'm not sure what else he said. I know he never raised his voice—that it remained level and cold, every word flicking like a lash. And somehow I knew that that was the end of Wally Jordan. That he had not been shrewd, as he had thought, in trying to discredit Uncle George and his ideas by discrediting Joey, but very foolish. That even if Uncle George had not said what he was saying, as soon as everyone in the auditorium—and everyone in the town—had had a chance to think about it, they would have turned against Jordan. But I didn't care about that, and I couldn't think about it at the moment. All I could think of was Joey—of the lost, stricken expression on his face.

I don't cry easily. I only remember crying twice before that: when Dad died and later when Mother did. But I cried now, cried with the same sense of loss that I had felt then, and with the pain that comes with the knowledge that you have inflicted pain on someone you love.

I'm not sure whether it was his hand on my shoulder or his saying, "Don't, Mark," that made me stop. I wiped my eyes, looked at him. He was looking at me, and though his expression was grave, searching, it was no longer lost, hurt to the point of shocked numbness. Then suddenly he smiled his slow warm smile, a smile of relief as well as love, and I knew that now he understood what I had done and why.

"I'm sorry, Joey," I began.

"No," he said. "You were right—right about that and about a lot of other things."

"What other things?"

"About the white pigeon. And about people. I've got a lot to learn—how to talk and think and act like everyone else. And about baseball, basketball, football and things like that too."

"It might help," I admitted. "At least . . ."

"It won't just help," he said. "It's terribly important. Because the more I learn about other people now, the better we'll be able to do later on."

"We?"

He looked at me in surprise. "Do you think I can do any of the things I'd like to do alone? I'm always going to need you, the way I needed you just now. Of course, you've got to be sure you're interested . . ."

He broke off. I didn't say anything, but I didn't have to. He knew.

Gilly Ground was an orphan and all he wanted was a little peace and quiet . . .

DORP DEAD

by Julia Cunningham

illustrated by James Spanfeller

Life in the orphanage was difficult in many ways. Gilly spent as much time as he could in the abandoned tower in the woods. It was peaceful there—and it was there that Gilly met the Hunter. Then, one day, he was placed in a foster home. And Gilly felt as though he were trapped in a nightmare come true.

An Avon Camelot Book
51458 $1.95

Also by Julia Cunningham
DEAR RAT   46615 $1.50